To my parents,
Hattie and John Springer
a very special couple

CRY UNCLE!

Mary Jane Auch

A BANTAM SKYLARK BOOK®
NEW YORK • TORONTO • LONDON • SYDNEY • AUCKLAND

This edition contains the complete text
of the original hardcover edition.
NOT ONE WORD HAS BEEN OMITTED.

RL 5, 008–012
CRY UNCLE!

A Bantam Skylark Book / published by arrangement with
Holiday House, Inc.

PRINTING HISTORY
Holiday House edition published 1987
Bantam edition / March 1990

Skylark Books is a registered trademark of Bantam Books, a division of Bantam Doubleday Dell Publishing Group, Inc. Registered in U.S. Patent and Trademark Office and elsewhere.

All rights reserved.
Copyright © 1987 by Mary Jane Auch.
Cover art copyright © 1990 by Lino Saffiotti.
Library of Congress Catalog Card Number: 87-45330.
No part of this book may be reproduced or transmitted in any form or by any means, electronic or mechanical, including photocopying, recording, or by any information storage and retrieval system, without permission in writing from the publisher.
For information address: Holiday House, Inc., 18 East 53rd Street, New York, NY 10022.

ISBN 0-553-15787-6

Published simultaneously in the United States and Canada

Bantam Books are published by Bantam Books, a division of Bantam Doubleday Dell Publishing Group, Inc. Its trademark, consisting of the words "Bantam Books" and the portrayal of a rooster, is Registered in U.S. Patent and Trademark Office and in other countries. Marca Registrada. Bantam Books, 666 Fifth Avenue, New York, New York 10103.

PRINTED IN THE UNITED STATES OF AMERICA

CWO 0 9 8 7 6 5 4 3 2 1

ABOUT THE AUTHOR

MARY JANE AUCH is the author of several books for young readers, including two future titles for Bantam Skylark Books, *Mom Is Dating Weird Wayne* and *Pick of the Litter*. *Cry Uncle!*, her first novel, was awarded the 1986 work-in-progress grant by the Society of Children's Book Writers. It has also been nominated for the 1989–90 Mark Twain Award (Missouri) and the 1989–90 Virginia State Reading Association Young Readers Award.

A free-lance writer and illustrator, the author also works part-time as a writing teacher and library volunteer. Mary Jane Auch lives with her husband and two grown children on a small farm near Rochester, New York. The author spent several years "experimenting" with farm living and claims that the wheat-threshing and bread-baking incidents in *Cry Uncle!* really happened. "I'm still using some of the hard loaves as doorstops!" she jokes.

and cheered. Now I could see why she'd been grand champion of the bus rodeo for five years in a row.

There was a big JUST MARRIED sign on the back of the bus, and somebody had tied a whole bunch of old shoes to the back bumper. They drove back past the crowd one more time before heading out of the parking lot. Uncle Will was grinning and clapping his hands in time to the horn.

"Do you think he's Uncle Will or Willie right now?" Sara whispered.

"Who cares?" I said. "Whoever he is, he's happy."

CRY UNCLE!

Chapter 1

I pressed my face to the school bus window so I could see down the road to the spot where I was usually ambushed, halfway between our farm and the bus stop at the next corner. Rats! They were there again. The Spider Twins were lurking in the bushes, waiting for me.

They were really named Snyder, and Leo was fourteen, a year older than Lester, but everyone had trouble telling them apart. They were the ugliest kids I'd ever seen, with pasty white faces, stringy black hair, beady little eyes, and long spidery arms and legs.

They had spotted me as a sucker from the first day we moved to Adams, about three weeks ago. I was the second shortest boy in the sixth grade and no match for the Spiders, even though I'd been sneaking workouts every day with my brother's E-Z Pump-Up Muscle Builder. The TV ad said it was supposed to turn your muscles into coiled springs, but so far mine were more like rubber bands.

When the bus was almost to my stop, I noticed Sara Weiderman, another sixth-grader, sitting a few seats ahead of me. That gave me an idea. Sara lived around the corner, about a quarter of a mile down Berg Road, and the Weiderman's property backed up to our woods. I slid into the seat next to her.

"Hey, Sara," I whispered. "Can I get off at your house today?"

She looked at me like I had a live tarantula on my head. "Why?"

"Look, I'm not going to hang around or anything. I just want to get off there and cut back through the woods to my house."

"Why?" she repeated.

The school bus brakes were starting to squeal, so I knew I was running out of time.

"Listen, Sara. It's an emergency. I'll tell you about it after we get off."

"What kind of emergency?"

"The Spider Twins are waiting to jump me if I get off at my own stop."

"Oh. Okay," she said. She finally understood. All the kids knew about the Spider Twins.

When the bus stopped, I tried to slide down in my seat, so Mrs. Guptill, our bus driver, wouldn't see me, but she spotted me in her rear-view mirror. "Wake up, Anderson. This is your stop," she bellowed.

I ran up to the front of the bus to plead my case. The kids called Mrs. Guptill "the water buffalo" behind her back. She ran her bus like a cell block, and just wasn't the kind of driver you shouted explanations to from the rear of the bus.

Mrs. Guptill was one of the few drivers in our school district who owned her own bus, so she could fix it up any way she wanted to. It looked like a regular school bus from the outside, but on the inside it was a whole different world. Mrs. Guptill had painted a huge rainbow that arched from the back seat up over the ceiling to the front. There were clouds painted here and there on the ceiling, labeled *cirrus*, *cumulus* and *cumulonimbus*, and in the spaces between those, she had put in the constellations. On the partitions between the windows, she had painted the bird and flower of each state, along with the date that state entered the union. She wasn't a terrific artist, but you could tell what everything was, especially since it was labeled. On the back of the seats, she had lettered weekly spelling lists, starting with first grade in the front and ending up with sixth grade in the back. Addition, subtraction, multiplication, and division tables ran around the whole bus on the strip just above the windows. Mrs. Guptill's bus was probably the only one in the whole school that the kids didn't mess up with graffiti. She hadn't left any room for it.

"I'm supposed to go to Sara's house today, Mrs. Guptill," I said, casually reaching out for the peppermint-striped pole behind her seat.

She blew a stray hunk of hair out of her eyes and held out her big paw.

"So where's your bus pass?"

I could feel my face getting red. Stupid Dora Simpson from my class was sitting in the front seat giggling and whispering to the girl next to her.

"My mom forgot to give me one," I explained. "But she wants me to go to Sara's. Honest!"

"Yeah? So why did I see her car in the driveway

if she's not home?" Old Guptill should have been a detective.

"Oh, Mom is home, Mrs. Guptill, but she has a bunch of her friends over this afternoon and I'm not supposed to butt in. That's why she wants me to stay at Sara's until she comes to pick me up."

Mrs. Guptill looked at me for a few seconds with the kind of squinty-eyed stare that made me feel she was reading my mind. I tried to fake her out with mental telepathy. *Look at the boy's face. You can tell he's honest*. The water buffalo saw right through me.

"Funny, there were no extra cars in the driveway. Just the one. I suppose your mother's friends just walked over, huh? Only five houses per mile on this road, but all those nice ladies just jumped into their hiking boots and came for tea." This got a big laugh from the whole front of the bus.

"I think Mom was going to pick them up," I mumbled. Dora Simpson let out a horse laugh and threw her head back so far her glasses fell off.

Mrs. Guptill slapped her big hand down on the door-opening lever.

"No bus pass, no side trips. This ain't no tour bus I'm running here. Nice try though, Anderson."

I went slowly down the steps and the door thunked behind me. I watched as the words "Guptill Transit Co.—Mabel Guptill, President, Vice-President, Driver, and Decorator" moved slowly past me, right at eye level. Then I took a deep breath and braced myself for the attack of the Spiders.

Mom told me I should always walk down the road facing traffic, but that meant I'd have to go by the bushes where the Spiders were waiting. I decided that getting hit by a car wouldn't be a whole lot worse than being beat up, so I crossed to the other side. I avoided looking across the road and pretended to be real interested in the field on my right, hoping they wouldn't notice me.

"Hey, stupid!"

I didn't look up.

"Hey you, city kid!"

"Who? Me?" I tried to look amazed that they would be calling to me.

"Yeah, you. You see any other kids over there, dummy? C'mere." Lester was the one doing the talking. Or was it Leo?

"Can't. I gotta get right home."

The other Spider spoke up. "You ain't gonna make it home at all if you don't get over here right now."

I gauged the distance to our house, but knew I couldn't outrun the Spiders from here. I was pretty fast in a short sprint, but those long spider legs could overtake me in no time at all. I crossed the road slowly, hoping a truck might hit me before I got to the other side.

The one in the red shirt grabbed the collar of my jacket, pulling me back into a small clearing behind the bushes. "What's in your pockets?"

"Nothing, honest."

"The little brat's lying, Leo," said the one in the black shirt. He had to be Lester. He had a longer nose than Leo. Maybe I could tell them apart after all. Leo yanked off my jacket and started going through my pockets. In the past three weeks, they had ripped off the change from my lunch money four times and had taken my Yankees cap, a pack of gum, some fireballs, and a laser sticker. Today I wised up. I took exact change for lunch and didn't carry anything the Spiders might want to steal.

"Empty," Leo growled, throwing my jacket on the ground and grinding it into the dirt with his foot. I was going to catch it from Mom when she saw that jacket. "What about your other pockets? Take off your jeans."

"No way," I said.

"Oh, yeah?" Leo grabbed my arm and in one quick move twisted it around and pushed it up against my back.

"Owww! Cut it out."

"Not till you cry uncle and take off your jeans."

"No!"

"Oh, yeah? How about now?"

He gave another shove, and I thought my arm was going to come right off at the shoulder.

"Uncle!" I yelled, understanding for the first time why spies give up their secrets.

Leo kept pushing. "What about the pants?"

"No way. I'm not taking off my pants," I squeaked.

Leo pulled my other arm behind my back, and the two of them wrestled me to the ground.

Lester undid my pants and yanked them off my legs. Then he started going through the pockets, while I scrunched up on the ground like an idiot, trying to cover up my underwear.

"He ain't got nothin' in here neither," Lester said, jamming his fist into the last of the pockets. He tossed my jeans to Leo and started back out to the road. Leo kicked a cloud of dust into my face. "Too bad you didn't have nothin' for us today, stupid. Be sure you do next time. Hey, Lester! Wait up," he yelled, running to catch up to his brother.

I followed them out to the edge of the bushes to see where they had dropped my pants. The two Spiders were loping down the road, my jeans stretched between them like a sail. I couldn't believe it. I'd have to go home in my underwear.

I picked up the jacket and tied it around my waist with the flap in back. It covered up the back all right, but the ends of the tied sleeves didn't do much in the way of hiding my front. I switched it around so the flap was in front, but I could tell from the draft that the back was pretty much out in the open.

Finally, I had the brilliant idea of putting the jacket on upside down like a pair of pants. I put my feet through the sleeves and pulled them up. The shoulders came just above my knees. I zipped up the front and pulled the material tight around my waist. There was a hole by my knees where the neck was supposed to be, but I could keep it closed by squeezing my knees together. The overall effect wasn't terrific, because, for one thing, the jacket was bright orange. Practically glow-in-the-dark orange. Mom bought it because she didn't want anybody mistaking me for a deer when I went into the woods during hunting season. The way she acted, you'd think I was planning on wearing antlers. Anyway, as weird as the upside-down jacket looked, it was better than running down the road in my Fruit of the Looms.

After checking up and down the road for cars, I started out. It wasn't easy trying to run with my knees locked together, so I did a kind of sideways, hunched over, knock-kneed gallop. All I needed to do was let my arms dangle down, and I would've looked like a chimpanzee.

I was making pretty good progress when I noticed a car coming toward me. There was nothing but open field on either side of the road now, so I tried to speed up. If I could just get to the beginning of our property, I could dive into the grove of sumac trees by the road. The car was coming pretty fast, so I tried to take bigger steps. Instead of moving faster, I felt my knees were suddenly caught in a lasso. I fell flat on my face and rolled into the ditch. The driver of the car saw me fall and came to a gravel-spitting stop just across the road from me. I kept my head down, hoping they would go away.

A woman's voice called out. "Davey? Davey Anderson, is that you?"

I peeked over the edge of the ditch. Geez! Why did it have to be her? It was Mrs. DelVecchio, the music teacher, the only really pretty teacher I'd ever had in my whole life. And here I was wearing a neon-orange jacket for pants. I knelt, making sure my bottom was hidden from view. "Yeah, it's me, Mrs. DelVecchio."

"Are you hurt?"

"No. I'm just checking out something down here in the ditch for a science project."

"Really? It looked as if you fell."

"Oh, gee, no. I just noticed this endangered species of weed all of a sudden. I probably ducked in here kind of fast because it's a rare find."

Mrs. DelVecchio didn't look convinced, but she

smiled. She was beautiful when she smiled. "Well, if you're sure you're all right."

"Oh, yeah. I'm great, honest. I do stuff like this all the time. I'm a real science freak." Why couldn't I be wearing normal clothes? Then I could moan and groan like I'd been hit by a car and Mrs. DelVecchio would come running over to give me first aid. Maybe even mouth-to-mouth resuscitation.

"I see. Well, I'll see you tomorrow, Davey."

"Sure. Goodbye, Mrs. DelVecchio." I watched her drive away. I'd had a few daydreams about meeting Mrs. DelVecchio outside of school, but this wasn't the way I'd imagined it. Not by a long shot.

Chapter 2

I ran down the road and dove into the shelter of the sumac grove, then followed the hedgerow that curved around behind our barn. It was slow going, because there were about a million wild blackberry bushes, catching me with their thorns as I pushed my way through. From the barn, I had to make a run for it to the back of the house. I ducked behind the porch without being seen and sneaked over to peek in the kitchen window.

Brad, my older brother, was sitting at the table, wolfing down his usual after-school snack—three bowls of cereal. Mom was across from him, and they seemed to be arguing. I couldn't go in through the kitchen, but I figured the argument would keep them occupied enough so they wouldn't see me climb the rose trellis and go across the porch roof to the upstairs hall window. I ducked under the window to get to the trellis, but when I tried to step on the first rung, the jacket wouldn't stretch far enough. I knew I'd have to take it off in order to make the climb. I checked to see if anybody was watching. There were a couple of hens scratching around under the lilac bush. Other than that, the coast was clear.

I slipped out of the jacket and started the climb in my underwear. I hoped whatever Mom and Brad were fighting about would hold Brad's attention, because from where he was sitting, he could see the top of the trellis. The trellis was shaky, and I was getting scratched up pretty bad by the thorns. Then, when I was almost to the top, the trellis started to sway and pull away from the house. I held my breath and hung on for all I was worth. Gradually the swaying trellis reversed direction and smacked up against the house again. I scrambled to safety and tiptoed across the porch roof to the hall window. It was open, so I just had to slide the screen up and climb in.

I could hear Mom and Brad still arguing as I crept down the hall to my room. I pulled on my other pair of jeans and sneaked down the stairs and out the front door, which was only locked from the outside. Then I walked in the kitchen door as if I were just getting home from school. I was pretty sure Brad hadn't seen me, or he would have made a big deal about it in front of Mom. Brad liked getting me in trouble. In his mind, he was only paying me back because I kept him from achieving his major goal in life—to be an only child.

Just as I came through the door, Brad dropped the bomb. He looked straight at me and said, "There's no way I'm living in the same house with somebody who runs around in broad daylight with no clothes on."

I stopped dead. My big "Hi, I'm home" smile

stayed pasted across my face as I stared at Mom's back. A million excuses about losing my pants were running around inside my head, bumping into each other. Like: *There was this really poor kid sitting next to me on the bus with these really ragged pants on and I felt sorry for him so I gave him my pants.* Or maybe: *I was running down the road and the zipper must have busted loose because the pants just fell right off, and when I went back to look for them, they were gone.*

It was no use. There was no logical explanation for coming home without my pants. Even if I could tell the truth and say I was mugged—which I couldn't because the Spiders had said they would poison our dog and burn down our barn if I squealed—Mom wouldn't believe me. One of the main reasons why she wanted us to move to the country in the first place was to get away from muggers.

When Mom turned to look at me, she was smiling. That was a bad sign. She probably thought I'd gone nutso, and she was going to stay nice and calm until she could call somebody to haul me off to the funny farm.

Brad made things worse, as usual. "When people go off their rocker, they should be in a nuthouse, not living with normal people, for pete's sake."

"Come over and sit down, Davey," Mom said. She turned back to Brad, picked up a long, thin zucchini from the pile on the table, and pointed it at him. "You keep your opinions to yourself, Brad. I want to talk to your brother."

I slid into the seat next to Mom. Her *One Hundred and One Imaginative Ways to Use Zucchini*

are complaining about him running around stark naked, that's why," Brad said.

Naked! So Brad hadn't been talking about me after all. I'd made it into the house without being seen. I sat back in my chair, letting the feeling of relief wash over me.

Mom was still going on about Uncle Will. "You're not being fair, Brad. Uncle Will got confused just that once and happened to go out of the house without getting dressed."

"Honest?" I asked. "He went out naked?"

"As a jaybird!" Brad said, tilting back in his chair, laughing. "Except for his shoes and socks. He passed three other farms and a gas station before they nailed him." I couldn't help laughing myself.

"Stop it, both of you," Mom said. "I won't have you making fun of Uncle Will. He's not crazy. This all started after Uncle Ray's funeral. It was too much of a strain for Uncle Will to stay on the farm alone, trying to keep things going all by himself. And he missed his brother so much."

"Is he going to get better?" I asked. "Could somebody move in with him so he wouldn't be so lonesome?"

Brad snorted, but Mom ignored him and turned to me. "We thought of that, Davey, but the area where he lives is so remote, there just isn't anybody. The neighbors could check in on him once in a while, but he needs more than that, even though he isn't confused all the time."

Brad let his chair fall back into place with a bang. "What Mom is leading up to is that the old coot is going to come live with us."

"Here?" I asked.

"No, in Cleveland," Brad said, rolling his eyes.

I wanted to tell Mom I was having enough trouble trying to fit into a new school, where nobody particularly liked me and the Spiders hated me, without adding a naked old uncle to the picture, but I could see the tears in her eyes, so I kept quiet.

The tears didn't stop Brad. "Why don't we just put up a big sign out front that says 'Anderson Loony Bin and Nudist Colony'? Then we could attract all the nuts in Wayne County and make the old geezer feel right at home," he said.

"That does it," Mom shouted, winging a zucchini at Brad. He ran out of the room, so it missed him and skidded across the floor, bouncing off the refrigerator and spinning slowly to a stop in the middle of the kitchen, like a fat green propeller. Mom had just discovered the one hundred and second imaginative way to use zucchini.

Chapter 3

We pulled into the circular driveway at the farm, right behind a big truck labeled COLONEL CHARLES HOFFSTETTOR'S AUCTION SERVICE. Two men were hauling a beat-up old sofa into a tent on the front lawn. Some other guys were dragging farm tools from the barn.

Mom started crying as soon as she got out of the car. Dad tried to put his arm around her, but she shook her head and headed for the house. Dad followed her, and I tagged along. "I know you're upset, Jan, but it can't be helped. We'll be lucky if the auction brings in enough to cover the debts from this place. Lord knows the old man couldn't keep it going even when he was in his right mind and there were two of them to share the work."

Mom turned and glared at Dad over a soggy Kleenex. "Stop referring to him as the old man, John. He's a person. He has a name." She pushed the door open.

"All right, I'm sorry. But my point is that you can't hang on to a dying farm just because the family has always owned it and you have fond memories of coming to it as a child."

"Those are the very best reasons for hanging on to a dying farm," Mom said. "Quite possibly the only reasons." She went into the house, slamming the door hard.

Dad started to reach for the doorknob, then shrugged. When he turned around, I realized I was standing with my mouth hanging open. Mom and Dad hardly ever argued.

Dad put his arm around me. "Don't worry about your mother, Davey. She knows we're doing what needs to be done, but if she had her way, we'd have two play farms in the family instead of just one."

Dad had started calling our place "the play farm" after the first week we'd been there. The moving-out-of-the-city plan had been Mom's idea, but Dad had gone along with it. I think she convinced him by using guilt about us kids—cleaner air, better schools, more room to grow, and stuff like that. Mom had even tried to get Dad into the spirit of the thing by buying him one of those plaid flannel farmer's shirts. The first time he put it on, he wore a tie with it. Mom had a fit! Poor Dad was "city" right down to his bones.

We could hear Mom going from room to room, calling to Uncle Will. Dad undid the top button of his farmer's shirt (no tie today) and wandered over to look at the junk in the auction tent. I took off to explore by myself.

I didn't exactly remember being at the farm before, but there was something familiar about the place. I started to go into the barn nearest the house, but a guy carrying out a big carton nearly knocked me over. "Watch out, kid. Hey, Charlie? Where do you want this junk?"

A man in a white cowboy hat came over and poked around in the box. He shook his head. "Stuff looks pretty useless to me. Be lucky if we can get fifty cents for the lot."

"That's the trouble with these crazy old coots," the other one answered. "They never throw anything away."

It made me mad to hear them talking about Mom's uncle like that. He might be crazy now, but the stories Mom told us on the trip to the farm made it sound like he was a pretty nice guy when he was younger. Too bad Brad wasn't along to hear all that. He had to work Saturday mornings, so he stayed home. He probably would've made a lot of nasty remarks anyway. Brad was really mad about having to share his room with me after Uncle Will moved in. I wasn't so wild about the idea myself.

I heard a lot of squawking going on and followed the noise back to a second barn. Some men were bringing chickens out and shoving them into wooden crates. Each man carried a chicken in each hand, holding it upside down by the legs. The air was full of dust and feathers. The way the men were running down the ramp, with the chickens flapping their wings, it looked like they were experimenting with a new way to fly.

I was so busy watching the launch of the chicken men, I didn't see him at first. He was leaning against a wooden fence, his hands jammed into the pockets of blue farmer's coveralls. He was a lot older than the pictures and the smile was gone, but you could still see the crinkles it had left around his eyes. His eyes weren't laughing anymore, though.

I didn't realize I was staring at him until he said, "What's the matter? You never saw a crazy person before? That's what they're callin' me, you know—crazy!"

I looked away and pretended I hadn't heard him.

"You boy! Come over here."

I couldn't think of a way out, so I walked over to him. He jerked his head toward the chicken men. "That is what it all comes to in the end, boy. You work real hard until your life is almost over. Then they come and steal it all away from you and use fancy lawyers to make it nice and legal."

He turned and gripped the top rail of the fence so hard his knuckles got white. "Take my advice, boy. Don't work hard. Be a bum. The bums are the smart ones. They know. Yessir, they know, all right. We all come out even in the end."

He sure sounded crazy, and he was looking off toward the meadow, so I wasn't sure whether he was talking to me or not. Then he tilted his head back and peered at me through the bottoms of his glasses. The thick glass made his eyes look big and bugged out. "Who are you, anyway, boy?"

"I'm Davey," I said, feeling uneasy under his stare.

"Who?"

"Davey. Your niece, Jan, is my mother."

"You're Jan's boy? Why didn't you say so in the first place? You've growed some since I saw you last. How old are you now?"

"Eleven."

He looked me up and down for a minute, nodding his head. "You remember when you came here to visit us?"

I didn't want to hurt his feelings. "I . . . uh . . . sort of, I guess."

"Don't remember a durn thing about it, do you. You was too young. Come with me. I'll show you something." He started off on a path that wound up through the meadow. I wasn't so sure I wanted to follow him. He stopped and turned, realizing I wasn't behind him. "What's the matter? You believe them stories? You afraid to go off with your crazy uncle?"

"No sir," I lied. I knew Mom wanted us to be nice to him, so I ran to catch up.

He didn't walk like an old man. He swung his right leg with a little hitch, but he took long steps and moved fast. It wasn't that easy to keep up with him.

"Where are we going?" I asked.

"You'll see. You'll remember, too. I'll bet you a nickel."

Yeah, sure, I thought.

"Here, you'll be needing this." He reached down in his pocket and pulled out a filthy piece of stale bread. Geez! This guy really was a loony. I sure wasn't going to eat it, but I thought I should humor him.

"Thanks." I pretended to break off a piece and put it in my mouth.

He knocked my hand away. "What are you, crazy, boy? Your mother don't feed you enough?"

Now I didn't know what he expected of me.

Maybe that was what it would be like, living with a crazy person. He could just make up the rules as he went along, but I'd never know what game we were playing. As he led me farther and farther down the path, I though about leaving a trail of bread crumbs.

All of a sudden, we came over a rise and I saw the pond, a beautiful round little pond with weeping willow trees around it and, in the center, a white swan.

Something clicked inside my head. "I remember that swan," I whispered.

"Thought you would."

"Why?"

"Because you and I spent a whole afternoon and half a loaf of bread feeding that swan. I practically had to drag you out of here when it was time to go back."

A picture of Uncle Will's laughing face against a summer blue sky flashed through my mind. I could see the two of us tossing bread to the swan, trying to coax it to glide closer to the shore where I could reach out to it with baby hands. "Yeah, I remember," I said.

Uncle Will's face crinkled up into his old one-sided grin. "You owe me a nickel, boy."

Chapter 4

By the time we got back to the house, Mom and Dad had already packed Uncle Will's suitcase and cartons in the back of the station wagon. Mom came toward us, reaching out her arms to Uncle Will. Her face screwed up like a little kid's, and she cried into his shoulder when she hugged him. He patted her back and said, "It's all right, Janny girl. It's all right." But you could tell from the look in his eyes, it wasn't all right at all.

Dad just stood there shifting uncomfortably from one foot to the other. He glanced at his watch. "It's getting near time for the auction. Maybe we'd better get out of here before the car gets blocked in."

Mom blew her nose and put on a phony cheerful smile. She followed Uncle Will as he wandered into the tent to look over his stuff one last time. He sat down in an old stuffed leather chair and rubbed his hand on the arm of it, as if he were petting a dog. I thought Mom was going to start bawling all over again.

"Don't suppose you'd have room to bring this along, would you?" Uncle Will asked.

Mom's voice was low and husky. "Sure, Uncle Will."

Dad sized up the chair. "The auctioneer must have it on his list by now. I'm not sure he'll be willing to give it up."

Uncle Will looked Dad straight in the eye. "The auctioneer ain't the one who's giving things up here."

Dad's face turned red. "Oh, sure. Well, I didn't mean . . . just thought . . ." His voice sort of trailed off.

Uncle Will got up and walked slowly past the junk-covered tables, finding a few more things he couldn't part with. He never even bothered to check with the auctioneer. Dad rearranged everything in the back of the station wagon so we could fit in the old chair. We took off just as the first people were starting to arrive for the auction.

Uncle Will was quiet after that. He just sat staring out of the window. A couple of times he reached up as if to touch something as we drove past it, then let his hand slide down the glass and drop back into his lap. After a while, he just looked straight ahead and didn't say anything, unless Mom turned around to ask him a direct question. Mom was running off at the mouth, trying to be real cheerful, but she wasn't fooling anybody. It only made the whole thing seem sadder.

After about a hundred years, we pulled into the driveway at home. Mom dragged Uncle Will off on a tour of the farm while I helped Dad get the stuff into

Uncle Will's new room. We saved the chair for last, which was a mistake, because it got wedged on the stair landing and we couldn't budge it either way.

"Brad!" Dad yelled. "Come here and give us a hand."

Brad came out of his room—*our* room now. He looked down over the upstairs railing at the mangy old chair.

"Where the heck are you going with that ugly thing, Dad?"

"Never mind the editorial comments, Brad. Just see if you can get below the chair with Davey and give it a good shove. I can't do it by pulling."

Brad climbed over the railing and hung by his hands for a second, then swung his legs and dropped down on the step next to me. Brad was always able to do neat stuff like that. He was over six feet tall and a big-shot athlete.

"Move over, short stuff," he said, getting a good grip on the seat of the chair. "Geez! This thing stinks, Dad. Smells like cat pee."

"Just push, Brad," Dad said, "We'll get it cleaned up later."

Brad gave it a shove that almost knocked Dad over, but the chair came loose, and we took it on up the stairs. The only problem was, no matter how hard we tried to shift things around in the room, the leather chair wouldn't fit in. Uncle Will was getting my room, the smallest in the house. Brad's room was bigger, so the two of us could fit into it better. Actually, Brad and I needed a room about the size of

The Florence W. Ungerman
Memorial Library
Cape Cod Academy

the school gym for him to think I wasn't crowding him.

"We'll have to find room for this downstairs," Dad said. "Uncle Will can sit in it to watch TV." Brad had disappeared, so the two of us lifted the big ugly chair and worked it back down the stairs without getting it hung up this time. By moving a few things around, we managed to fit it into the front corner of the living room, by the bookshelf. I moved the floor lamp over next to it.

"There," I said. "Now he can read in here too, if he wants to." I didn't mind that Uncle Will was coming to live with us, as long as he kept his clothes on. At least I wasn't as upset about it as Brad. Uncle Will didn't seem much crazier than a lot of other people I'd run into. Brad was right about the chair, though. It did smell like cat pee.

Mom had just come back from dragging Uncle Will all over the property, and now she was busy flitting around the kitchen. She had Uncle Will sitting at the table already. "Dinner will be ready in just a jiffy," she said, tying her hair back with a red bandanna.

Mom was getting a little carried away with some of this country stuff. She was dressing like a pioneer woman, and she'd fixed the whole house up in what she called "country style," with a lot of old things. They were supposed to be antiques, but they just looked beat up to me.

Mom pulled a casserole out of the refrigerator. "I knew we'd all be hungry as soon as we got back, so I made this ahead of time." It looked suspiciously green.

"What is it?" I asked.

"Zucchini Frittata Casserole," she said, beaming. "I'm just going to pop it in the microwave for five minutes, and we'll be ready to eat."

I swallowed hard and felt my stomach turn over. Uncle Will didn't look any more excited about the whole thing than I was.

"Brad must be upstairs," Mom said. "Davey, go tell him dinner's almost ready, will you?"

I went to the bottom of the stairs and had just taken a big breath to get ready to yell up to Brad, when Mom called out from the kitchen.

"Don't just stand there and shout, Davey. Go up the stairs."

I could never figure out how Mom did that. It was as if she could read my mind. I ran up the stairs and went into our room.

Brad was busy working at his computer, and he had the earphones on from his stereo. He was always plugged into so many circuits, I figured someday he'd blow a fuse in his brain. I tapped him on the shoulder, and he jumped about a mile.

"Did you ever hear of knocking?" he yelled.

"Yeah, I've heard of it, but I don't do it on my own door."

"What did you say?" Brad hadn't heard me because of the rock-music blasting in his ears.

"I just said I was sorry." I could be such a chicken sometimes. "Mom wants you to come downstairs. Dinner's ready."

"Yeah? Is it more of that zucchini junk?"

"I don't think so," I said. I wanted to enjoy the

look on Brad's face when he saw the goop we were getting tonight.

It was worth it. When Brad saw it, he turned almost as green as the casserole. Uncle Will was real quiet at dinner, especially after he had his first bite of the green stuff.

Mom kept running off at the mouth. "It's going to be just wonderful having you here, Uncle Will. We want you to think of this as your home now. You be sure to let us know if you need anything."

"Okay," Uncle Will replied.

"Here," Mom continued. "Have another helping of frittata. It's chock-full of vitamins. I want to fatten you up a little. You probably didn't cook much just for yourself, did you?"

Uncle Will was busy chewing, so he just shrugged.

Mom kept at him. "And don't feel you have to work around here. You deserve a good rest, so just feel free to sleep in in the mornings and nap in the afternoons, if you want to."

"Don't sleep much," he said. "Don't mind work, neither." He held up his hands to stop Mom from dishing him up another helping of the green goop.

Mom set down the casserole and patted Uncle Will on the shoulder. Her hands always reminded me of butterflies when she was getting uptight. "Oh, I never meant to imply that you couldn't . . . I mean that you aren't able to . . ."

Dad butted in. "Relax, Jan. Just let Uncle Will settle in the way he pleases. We're not going to force him to do anything he doesn't want to do." I thought it was funny that Dad talked *about* Uncle Will instead of *to* him.

Brad had given up on the main course. "Is there anything for dessert?"

"There certainly is," Mom said, jumping up to pull something out of the oven. "Zucchini cake."

Only eighty-five more imaginative meals to go. With any luck, the zucchinis would give out before we did.

Chapter 5

I was coming home on the school bus Monday, just minding my own business, when Sara Weiderman slid into the seat beside me.

"Did the Spiders get you on Friday?" she asked, looking straight ahead.

A picture of me running down the road in my jacket-pants flashed through my mind, and I could feel my face getting red. "Yeah," I mumbled.

"You get a bus pass from your mother today?"

"Naw. Mom asks too many questions. She'd want to know why, and call your mom and all. Besides if she ever found out about the Spiders, she'd probably go marching right over to talk to their parents."

"If the Spiders ever found out you squealed on them, they'd . . ." Sara made a slashing motion across her throat, complete with the sound of gushing blood, making it a little hard for me to swallow for a minute. We sat in silence, both staring ahead. Then Sara shoved a piece of paper into my hand. Before I could look at it or say anything else, Sara had moved to another seat. I unfolded the paper and read it.

Dear Mrs. Guptill,
From now on, Davey will be getting off the bus every day at Sara Weiderman's house. The address is 45 Berg Road. Thank you.
Sincerely yours,
Mrs. Anderson

From the handwriting you could swear it was written by an adult, but I knew Sara had done it. She was about the smartest person in the whole sixth grade. The teacher was always hanging her book reports up on the bulletin board because they were so neat. Another thing, it was really smart of Sara to think of using "Sincerely yours." I would've probably signed it "Your friend."

We were almost to my stop. I moved up into the seat behind Mrs. Guptill so I'd be ready to show her my bus pass. I studied the back of her head as she cruised down Lakeside. Her hair was brown, turning gray in little stripes. She pulled it up in a bun on top of her head, but pieces of it kept coming loose, so she had a kind of fringe over her face and neck.

I read the note again. Would the Water Buffalo see through it and humiliate me in front of the whole bus? Suddenly I realized we'd stopped. Mrs. Guptill had sighted me in her rear-view mirror. Talk about having eyes in the back of your head!

"You waitin' for an engraved invitation to get off, Anderson?"

"No Mrs. Wat . . . Mrs. Guptill. Here, I have this for you today." I shoved the note at her, trying not to look nervous.

"Givin' me love notes now, Anderson?" she asked, holding it at arm's length to read it.

Mrs. Guptill was the only person I knew who could play a whole comedy act with her back to the audience. I stood there sweating it out while she read the note. She kept blowing at a piece of hair that had come loose and landed on her nose. Each time she blew at it, it just came back to the same place again. She folded the note and put it in her pocket.

"Sit down, Anderson," she said, pulling the door level closed with a thunk. I almost fell back into my seat as the bus lurched forward. I couldn't believe it. She bought it! I sat there trying not to grin like an idiot as we rounded the corner onto Berg Road. When we stopped at Weiderman's farm, Sara walked past me and got off. I scrambled after her and went right up her driveway, so the Water Buffalo would think I was going into the house. I caught up to Sara just as she was going in the side door.

"Hey, thanks for the note, Sara," I said.

She just smiled and went inside. Sara wasn't much of a talker.

I found the path and headed into our woods. I felt terrific. No more run-ins with the Spiders. Sara had given me a permanent ticket to freedom. About halfway through the woods, I spotted our dog, Kaiser. I waved my arms around, trying to attract his attention, but he was on the scent of a rabbit and didn't see me. You couldn't yell to Kaiser because he was stone deaf. Dad always said he made a great watchdog, because all he could do was watch. He was also supposed to be a hunting dog, since he was a German short-haired pointer. But Kaiser had his own ideas about hunting, and they didn't involve running after some fool with a gun.

I finally gave up, and Kaiser went off on his own hunting trip. I had the feeling he'd seen me all along but was more interested in the rabbit than me. Kaiser just wasn't your basic "man's best friend."

I was almost to the part of the path I liked the best, the place where you could see the bridge over the creek, the pasture beyond it, and, in the distance, the back of our house. I still couldn't believe all this land belonged to us. Our old yard in the city would fit into our new place about a hundred times. I missed my friends, though.

I rounded the bend and saw Uncle Will standing on the bridge. "Hi," I called. "I'm home."

A big smile came over Uncle Will's face as he started toward me. At least somebody was glad to see me. "Ray? Is that you?" he asked, reaching out to me with both hands.

"It's me, Davey."

Uncle Will grabbed my arm. "Put your books down here, Ray. Let's hike over to Van Orden's farm and see the new colt."

"I'm Davey, Uncle Will."

"Davey?"

"I'm Jan's son. You're living here in Adams with us now."

Uncle Will rubbed his hand back and forth across his forehead. "Davey? But you look so much like Ray. I thought . . ." He dropped his hand, and his shoulders sagged as if he got real tired all of a sudden.

"Where is Ray?" he asked.

Geez! If he didn't remember his brother had

died, I wasn't about to be the one to tell him. Besides, I didn't have any idea how you were supposed to talk to him when he was acting crazy. All Mom had said was to be nice to him.

"Look, Uncle Will. Let's go back to the house and you can talk to Mom. She'll help you remember."

Uncle Will's face lit up again, and he looked back toward the house.

"Ma? Ma's here?"

"Not your ma, my ma."

Uncle Will's voice rose to a whine. "You and me got the same ma, Ray. Just because you're older don't give you no right to tease me, hear? If you're going to be mean, I'm going over to Van Orden's without you." He turned and headed back into the woods.

"Uncle Will, I'm sorry. Come on back," I yelled, but he just kept on walking. I needed help for sure now. Those woods went on for miles. I dropped my school stuff by the bridge and ran for the house. I burst through the screen door, letting it slam behind me. "Mom? Hey, Mom, where are you?"

No answer.

I ran up the stairs. "Mom? Come quick! Something's wrong with Uncle Will."

I stopped yelling long enough to listen. All I could hear was my own heartbeat and the ticking of the big grandfather clock down in the living room. I looked out the front bedroom window. The driveway was empty. Mom wasn't home. I ran back downstairs to look at the bulletin board.

Sure enough, there was a note: "Davey—I'm running errands. I'll be home by 4:30. Mom." I looked at the clock. That was almost an hour from now, and Mom was always twenty minutes later than she said she would be. Uncle Will could be in the next county by then.

I tried to think of somebody to call. Dad worked in Rochester, at least a half hour away, so he couldn't do any good. Brad had a basketball game in North Rose, so he wouldn't even make it home for supper. Other than that, I couldn't think of a single person I could call and say my crazy uncle was running away.

I took off out the door and ran for the woods. I hoped Uncle Will had stayed on the path. Even hunters who knew these woods got confused and ended up back on the road miles from where they thought they were. If Uncle Will thought he was someplace else to begin with, he could really get himself in a mess, especially if he started walking in circles.

"Uncle Will!" I yelled. "Uncle Will, do you hear me?" I stopped to listen, but all I could hear was the truck traffic from the main highway, a couple of miles away.

If Uncle Will thought he was a kid again, maybe I shouldn't be calling him uncle. What did Mom say they called him as a kid? Was it Willie? I tried it. "Willie! Willie, it's me, Ray!" Still no answer.

I was almost to the end of our woods. I could see Weiderman's barn through the trees. I followed the path up into Weiderman's driveway. There was no sign of Uncle Will, or anyone else, for that matter. That meant he'd probably wandered off the path somewhere in the woods. I ran out to look up and down the road just in case I was wrong. I could just barely make out a figure walking down the road. The sun was behind him, so I wasn't sure whether it was Uncle Will or not.

I started heading toward him. Pretty soon I could see more clearly. It was Uncle Will, all right. I could tell by the little hitch in his step. I wasn't close enough to call out yet, so I just kept going.

All of a sudden I saw the school bus coming down the road. Mrs. Guptill was finishing up her late run, which she did in the opposite direction, so she could end up at her house.

Uncle Will must have heard the bus behind him, because he turned around. Then he started waving his arms to flag it down. Geez! He was going to act like a fool in front of Mrs. Guptill. I'd never hear the end of this. Maybe she'd just keep going right by him. No—there were the yellow flashing lights, then the red ones. She was stopping for him.

I saw the bus door open and Uncle Will was saying something. I could tell because he was motioning with his hands. He was probably going through his little-kid routine with her. If the old Water Buffalo ever found out I was related to him, she could make my life miserable. I could just hear it now. "Hey, Anderson. How's your loony uncle? Is that where you get your absentmindedness from, Anderson?"

The red lights went off and the bus door closed. Uncle Will was on the bus. I ducked into some bushes as they got closer. When they went by, there was Uncle Will, with a big smile on his face, sitting right up front in the seat opposite Mrs. Guptill. He looked as if he thought he was on the way to school. Mrs. Guptill was laughing. At least there weren't any other kids on the bus. She must have dropped off the last of them before she picked him up.

As soon as they passed me, I ran as fast as I could to the corner. I got there just in time to see Mrs. Guptill pull away from our house. Uncle Will was standing in the driveway waving to her. That did it. I was ruined.

Chapter 6

Mom's car was in the driveway, so I ran inside and called to her, but there wasn't any answer. Then I looked through the kitchen window and saw her talking to Uncle Will. Great! If Mom heard Uncle Will talking like a little kid, I wouldn't have to explain everything to her. I went out to hear what they were saying.

Uncle Will's face looked different now, and his voice was back to normal. "Hello, Davey," he said. "Have a good day at school?"

"Uh . . . yeah . . . sure," I answered. He was pretending he didn't remember what happened before. And he didn't call me Ray.

"That's good," he said. "I never cared much for school when I was your age. Might have been better off if I'd paid more attention when I had the chance."

Was Uncle Will really crazy or just putting on an act? I had run around half the countryside looking for him, trying to keep him from getting lost. Now it seemed like the whole thing was some kind of stupid trick. I had to tell Mom what happened, as soon as I could get her alone. I didn't want to put up with any more of Uncle Will's nonsense. Crazy or not, he wasn't going to get away with it.

"Listen Mom, I need to talk to you, okay?"

"Sure, Davey, but will it keep for a few minutes? I want to get Uncle Will's advice about these hens." Mom's small flock of chickens were scratching around in the grass at our feet.

"I don't think so, Mom. I think we need to talk right now." I looked her right in the eye so she'd get the message.

"These girls ain't layin', are they?" Uncle Will said, watching the chicken that was pecking at his shoes.

"Why, no, they aren't," Mom said, turning her attention back to Uncle Will. She held up her index finger to me in her "just a minute" gesture, but I could tell Uncle Will had her hooked. Anything to do with the farm was the biggest thing in her life right now. "How did you know, Uncle Will?" she asked. "Can you tell that just by looking?"

"I can make a pretty good guess by looking. Can tell for sure by feeling, though." He scooped up the nearest hen and shoved her under his arm like a football. Then he poked his fingers around under her tail. He shook his head. "Where did you get these birds, anyway?"

"There was an ad in the *Penny Pincher*. The man I got them from said they'd been laying like crazy."

Uncle Will snorted. "Laying around is more like it. This hen hasn't had eggs on her mind for a good long time."

"Oh, Uncle Will, are you sure?" Mom asked.

"You don't think they're just taking a rest until they get used to their new surroundings?"

"I'm afraid not. Here, Jan. I'll give you a lesson in how to spot a lazy hen. See how many fingers you can fit between these pelvic bones."

Mom wrinkled up her nose and took a step back, pushing me forward. "Um . . . why don't you show Davey, Uncle Will? He can use the chickens as a 4-H project."

"No way," I said. "I'm not sticking my fingers up any chicken's—"

"Davey!" Mom cut me off. "Do what Uncle Will says. Maybe you'll learn something."

I made one quick poke at the hen and looked away fast.

"Did you feel that, Davey?" Uncle Will asked.

"Yeah," I lied.

"How many fingers?"

"I don't know. Three, maybe four, I guess." Geez. Who gave a hoot about a hen's pelvic bones anyway? Couldn't Mom see that this was just another of Uncle Will's crazy tricks?

Uncle Will practically pushed the hen into my face. "No, boy. You didn't feel it right. Try again. Feel for the two little pointy bones."

I looked at Mom. She raised one eyebrow, which meant I'd better do it or else, so I gritted my teeth and poked into the warm feathers. I almost threw up, but I found the bones. "They're close together," I said, gagging. "I can't fit any fingers between them."

Uncle Will smiled and let the hen go. "That's right. And a bird that's laying would have space for at least two or three fingers."

"That's really interesting, Uncle Will," Mom said. "Isn't that interesting, Davey?"

"Yeah, that's really interesting," I mumbled. Sure, easy for her to say. She didn't have to do any poking.

"Does this mean all the hens I bought aren't good for anything?" Mom asked.

"Didn't say that," Uncle Will said. "Just said they wouldn't be laying any more eggs. They'd make fine soup, though."

"You mean we have to kill them?" I asked.

Uncle Will grinned. "It's a lot easier to make the soup if you kill the chickens first. They don't always cooperate if you do it the other way around." He and Mom laughed, but I didn't think it was funny.

"I'm not sure I have the heart to kill them, Uncle Will," Mom said. "Maybe we could just keep them as pets."

"A chicken makes a mighty stupid pet," Uncle Will said.

Kaiser had found his way back from the woods and was standing like a statue, pointing at the chickens. For a few seconds he looked just like the cover picture on Dad's *Training Your German Short-Haired Pointer* book, but Kaiser's ear problem messed up his balance, and he couldn't stand on three legs for very long. Sure enough, he wobbled and fell over.

"We're used to stupid pets," I said.

"If you have a hatchet, Jan, I'll take care of those birds for you," Uncle Will said.

"No, I have to learn to do this myself, Uncle Will. I was just reading in *The Happy Homesteader* about how to kill a chicken in a humane way."

"Oh? How do you go about that?" Uncle Will asked.

"Let me see if I can remember. I read the article several times. It said something about . . . Wait here, I'll go find it." Mom ran back to the house, leaving me with Uncle Will.

Before I had a chance to get out of there, Uncle Will said, "Come here, boy. I'll show you some other ways to tell if a hen is laying or not."

"If it's all the same to you, Uncle Will, I think I've learned about all I'd ever want to know about chickens," I said. "The 4-H thing is Mom's idea, not mine."

Uncle Will shrugged. "Suit yourself."

There was an awkward silence. I wanted to say something to see if Uncle Will remembered what had happened back at the bridge.

"Did you find that farm?" I asked.

"What farm is that?"

"The Van-something-or-other farm. The place with the colt."

He squinted his eyes as if he were trying to remember. I would have pushed further, but the screen door slammed and Mom came out in the yard, flipping through the pages of a magazine.

"Here it is," she said, holding out the magazine to Uncle Will. "From Chicken Coop to Chicken Soup in Ten Easy Steps."

Uncle Will tilted his head back so he could look at the article through the bottoms of his glasses. "I don't know. Looks to me like city folks put this together, Jan."

"It makes a lot of sense, Uncle Will. Really, it

does. Now, let's see. 'Step one. Grasp the chicken by the neck.'" She grabbed for the nearest chicken, which took off with a lot of squawking.

"Have to catch 'em first," Uncle Will said. "Seems like they ought to make *that* step one."

Mom was chasing the chickens around the forsythia bush. "Don't just stand there, Davey. Help me!" I dove for three hens, but they scattered in all directions, leaving me with a small handful of tailfeathers. Uncle Will stood there for a while, watching us running around. Then he went over to the clothesline and took a wire hanger that was clipped to it. He untwisted the top of the hanger and began reshaping the wire.

Mom had stopped to catch her breath. "What are you going to do with that, Uncle Will?"

Uncle Will grinned. "If you want to catch a chicken, you have to be smarter than a chicken." With that, he snagged the leg of a hen with the wire loop he had made and picked her up so fast, we were more surprised than the chicken. He handed the bird to Mom. "Now you're ready for step one."

"Thanks, Uncle Will," Mom said. "All right, now. Step one. Let me just read this one more time."

"Mom, you're not really going to kill that thing, are you?" I asked. I couldn't believe she was going to go through with it. Mom had a hard time swatting a fly.

"It's not going to be bloody, Davey. Besides, if we're going to live on a farm, I have to learn to do these things. It's just a natural part of farm life." She swallowed a couple of times and took a deep breath. "Step two. Swing the bird over your head in three or four vigorous circles. The neck will snap, causing an instant and painless death."

Uncle Will shook his head. "I think the old hatchet method works better, Jan. I wouldn't put much stock in trying to swing a bird to death."

It was too late. Mom was already winding up. She closed her eyes and made three zinging circles over her head with the chicken. The wind rushing through the feathers made an incredible roaring sound, like a tornado. When Mom let go, the chicken dropped to the ground with a thud and just lay there. Never even made a squawk.

Mom opened her eyes, then started to cry. "Oh, the poor thing. I should have left it alone. Now it looks so pathetic, lying there like that."

She kneeled down and touched the bird's head. All of a sudden the chicken opened its eyes, blinked twice, then scrambled to its feet. Mom and the chicken stared at each other for a second or two. Then the chicken took off, running in little circles. Kaiser tried to point at it, but fell over right away. Uncle Will sat down on a bale of hay, threw back his head, and had a good laugh. As mad as I had been before, even I couldn't help laughing.

The hen made another pass by us, weaving first to one side, then the other. "That hen looks like a heavy drinker to me," Uncle Will said, wiping his eyes with a handkerchief.

"That does it," Mom said. "The next chicken who dies around here will have to commit suicide. I'm starting dinner." She stepped in the garden, plucked a few zucchinis, and headed for the house.

"Send that hen my way, Davey," Uncle Will said. "I want to see if she's hurt."

I went around behind the chicken and waved my arms to scare her over to Uncle Will. He snatched her up with the hook and ran his fingers down the feathers of her neck. "Looks like you're okay except for being scared half to death, old girl." He gently set the chicken down, and she ran off, clucking and ruffling her feathers.

I couldn't figure Uncle Will out. When he was talking about chickens, he didn't seem to be so crazy after all, at least not any crazier than Mom and her stupid magazine articles. Maybe he just got a little confused before, back at the bridge. After all, it takes a while to get used to living in a new place.

As we headed toward the house, Uncle Will stopped to look at the garden. We saw dozens of long green shapes lurking under the weeds and vines. "So this is where your mother's growing all those zucchinis," he said, tilting up a big floppy leaf with his foot.

"I don't think Mom's doing much about growing them," I said. "They seem to grow themselves."

Uncle Will nodded. "Zucchinis have a way of doing that."

I pictured each zucchini as another disgusting meal. It looked as if they might go on forever. "What makes them stop growing, Uncle Will?"

"The first killing frost ought to get rid of 'em."

"Is that going to be soon?" I asked.

Uncle Will put his arm around my shoulder and grinned at me.

"Not soon enough, Davey. Nowheres near soon enough."

Chapter 7

After supper that night I looked around for Mom. I'd kind of gotten over being mad at Uncle Will, but I still thought Mom should know what had happened that afternoon. I sure didn't feel like chasing after him again. Finally I spotted her in the back field by the creek, setting up the exercise bicycle in the bed of the pickup truck.

"Mom? Can we talk now?"

"Hmm?" Now she was piling bundles of tall grass into the truck bed. "Oh, Davey. I'm glad you came along. I can use your help. Get up on that bicycle, will you?"

I wasn't too wild about getting involved in Mom's projects. She'd had some pretty weird ideas since we moved to the farm.

"What are you trying to do, Mom?"

She held up a bunch of the grass. "Do you know what this is, Davey?"

"Grass."

"No, silly. It's wheat. It was just growing here in this field, and I thought it was weeds. Uncle Will pointed it out to me. The people we bought from must have planted it."

"Why do you want me on the bicycle?"

"The wheat needs to be threshed. That means separating the heads from the stems."

"With a bicycle?" I asked. I had the feeling this was going to be about as successful as the chicken killing.

"I'm sure this will work, Davey. Get up there and start pedaling. I'm going to push the ends of the wheat through the spokes of the rear wheel. It should take them right off."

"Look, I really need to talk to you, Mom."

"Fine, Davey. We'll talk while we work."

I climbed up on the bike and started cranking away. After I got some speed up, Mom pushed the first bunch of wheat into the spokes. I couldn't believe it. It worked like a charm. The heads of wheat separated from the stems and dropped on the tarp Mom had put in the truck. It sounded like a hailstorm.

I kept going for a few minutes, then I blurted it out. "I think maybe Brad is right about Uncle Will living here, Mom."

She kept watching what she was doing, which was a good thing, because she probably would've lost a finger if she'd looked up. "Why, Davey? Is something wrong?"

This wasn't the kind of talk I'd hoped for. We had to shout to each other over the noise of the bike.

"Well, yeah," I yelled. "He was kind of funny when I got home from school today."

"What do you mean, 'funny'?"

"He acted crazy, sort of. I mean, he thought he

was a little kid again, and he kept calling me Ray. He thought I was his older brother."

"That's to be expected, Davey. His brother's death came as such a shock. They'd lived together all their lives. Can you imagine how lost he feels? . . . Speed it up, Davey. The stems tangle in the spokes when you slow down. . . . His whole life has changed in the past few months. He was born in that old farmhouse and never left it until we brought him here. We have to help him forget all that. I'm sure he'll adjust to his new life with us, if we're patient."

"But Mom, he went running off to find some farm I never even heard of. I couldn't stop him. He thought he was home again—his old home."

"He ran off? Where? How did you get him to come back?"

I was getting out of breath. It was obvious I had the harder of the two jobs. "I didn't. By the time I ran to the house to find you, then went out again to look for him," I puffed, "he was all the way down Berg Road. And he flagged down the school bus to get home. Then, when I caught up with him, he was talking to you and acting normal."

Mom sat back and smiled. "Well, that just shows that his problem is a temporary one. If you hadn't left him alone, he probably would have come to his senses sooner. If it happens again, and you're the only one around, just stay with him and coax him back to the house." She jumped down off the truck bed to gather up the last few bunches of wheat.

"I don't know, Mom. There's an awful lot of places he could get lost around here. Maybe he'd be better off somewhere else."

"And just where would you suggest, Davey?" Mom snapped, throwing a load of wheat onto the truck bed. "We're all the family he has. If living with us doesn't work out, he'll have to go to a nursing home." She got back in the truck. "Start pedaling," she said, jamming the wheat into the wheel again.

I thought about the nursing home our scout troop visited last year for Christmas caroling. It smelled like the bus station men's room, and most of the people just sat around staring into space or mumbling to themselves. Uncle Will didn't belong in a place like that.

"I'm sorry, Mom. Maybe I shouldn't have said anything. It just scared me, that's all."

When Mom looked up, I could see tears in her eyes. "You didn't do anything wrong, Davey. Of course you had to tell me." She reached out and grabbed my ankle to stop me from pedaling. "Look," she shouted, then dropped her voice when the noise of the bike stopped. "I know this may not be easy, but I need your help to make things work with Uncle Will. Brad is being pigheaded about the whole thing, so I can't count on any cooperation from him. And your father. . . well, he's had reservations about having Uncle Will move in from the beginning, so I'd rather you keep things just between us for a while, okay?"

"Yeah, sure, Mom, but . . ."

"Look, Davey, all I can tell you is that Uncle Will is a wonderful man, and I want him to spend his last years with people who love him. I'd never even suggest that he stay here if I felt that he was in any way dangerous to himself or to us. Do you understand that?"

"Yeah, I guess so."

Mom smiled and wiped her eyes with the back of her hand. "I'll keep my eye on Uncle Will as much as I can. I'm home more than anyone else. Besides, he'll be a big help in teaching me about farm life. You saw how good he was with the chickens. As soon as he feels needed and wanted around here, I'm sure his periods of confusion will clear up."

"Okay, if you say so, Mom." I went back to my pedaling.

Just as we were finishing up the last of it, Uncle Will wandered out to see what we were doing.

"If anybody'd told me you could thresh wheat with a bicycle, I'd have laughed in his face," he said. "Got to hand it to you, Jan. You're mighty clever."

Mom smiled. "Thanks, Uncle Will. I'm pretty proud of the job myself. Can I grind this into flour now?"

Uncle Will picked up a handful of wheat and let it sift through his fingers. "You got to winnow it first. See? It still has the chaff in it, and bits of the straw."

"What's chaff?" I asked.

Uncle Will held out another handful of the grain to me, stirring it with his finger. "The outside of the wheat kernels that shattered off when you threshed it. You don't want that in the flour."

Mom slumped back against the tailgate. "I hadn't counted on this. How are we going to pick all those little bits and pieces out of there?"

"Won't have to," Uncle Will said. "The chaff is

lighter than the wheat, so you just need something to blow it away. Maybe a fan."

"We don't have a fan," Mom said. Then her face lit up. "I've got it. The wheat is already in the back of the truck. You know how windy the back of a pickup is when you drive down the road. Couldn't we blow it off that way?"

Uncle Will grinned. "If you could thresh it with that bicycle contraption, I don't see no reason why you couldn't winnow it out of the back of a truck. Let's give 'er a try. Better have Davey in the back to weigh down the tarp, though, or you'll lose the whole business."

We got the bike out of the truck, and Mom had me sit with my back up against the cab. "Here, Davey, spread your legs as wide as you can so you hold both sides of the tarp down."

She climbed into the driver's seat, and we drove slowly up the back field and out onto Lakeside. Then she turned onto Berg Road, which was straight and flat. There weren't any other cars in sight. Mom tapped on the back window. "You all set, Davey?"

"I guess so," I yelled.

Uncle Will hollered, "Let 'er rip!"

We took off down Berg Road, and the wheat chaff began swirling around me like a tornado. Within minutes, I had it in my mouth, my nose, and my ears. I banged on the back window, but Mom and Uncle Will didn't hear me because they were singing some old hymn called "Bringing in the Sheaves" at the top of their lungs.

I decided Uncle Will wasn't the only crazy one in the family. I also decided I'd ended up with the rotten part of the job again. By the time we got back home, the wheat looked terrific, but I was so covered with little bits of straw, they could've hung me up on a post and used me for a scarecrow.

Later that week, I stayed after school for intramurals, so I got home on the late bus. As I headed for my room, I could hear Uncle Will singing in the bathroom. He came out as I was walking by the door. The smell of after-shave just about knocked me over. He was wearing regular pants instead of his overalls, and his hair was all slicked back.

"I thought I heard a car pull into the driveway," he said. "Was it Mabel?"

"I didn't see anybody, Uncle Will."

He looked out the hall window. "Must be my ears are playing tricks on me. We should be able to hear Mabel real easy when she comes. She'll be on the bus."

I figured he'd gone loony on me again. The only bus that came out our way just went through the center of Adams on the main road. I thought about setting him straight, but I didn't feel like having an argument about it. I went on up to my room.

By the time I finished studying my spelling list, I decided I needed to get some nourishment to keep me going. I bumped into Uncle Will in the downstairs hall again.

"That must be her this time," he said. "Did ya hear the bus?"

"Look, Uncle Will. There aren't any buses out here, not on Lakeside, anyway. The bus route goes through the main part of town."

Uncle Will grabbed his sweater from the coat closet and stopped by the bathroom mirror to comb his hair again. "I'm not talking about that kind of bus, Davey. You know. . . Mabel's bus."

I'd been right before. It was easier to play along with him. "Oh, yeah," I said. "Mabel's bus comes by here all the time. Sometimes, two, three times a day." Geez! Pretty soon he'd have little green men in flying saucers stopping by to pick him up. I was about to go into the kitchen when we heard the squeal of brakes and a horn honking.

Uncle Will ran to the window. "There she is. Do I look good enough?" He was buttoning up his sweater, but he had missed the top button so it was all crooked.

"Yeah, you look fine, but your buttons are screwed up."

He tried to fix the buttons, but he skipped another one and made things worse.

"Hold still a second, Uncle Will. I'll straighten them out for you." I undid a couple of buttons and got them lined up.

Uncle Will ran in to take one more look in the mirror. What the heck was wrong with him? I'd never seen him even glance in a mirror before. "Thanks, Davey. Come on out with me and say hello to Mabel."

"Mabel who?"

"Your bus driver. Mrs. Guptill."

I looked out the window. Our whole driveway was filled with a very familiar-looking school bus.

"Oh . . . *that* Mabel."

I tried to think of an excuse, but he had a grip

on my arm and was dragging me through the kitchen. He was really strong for an old guy. Before I could make a run for it, somebody banged on the door.

When Uncle Will opened it, there was Mrs. Guptill with a big smile on her face. "You all set, Will? The movie doesn't start until six, so we have time to grab a bite somewhere first."

"Sounds just fine to me, Mabel. You know my grand-nephew Davey, don't you?"

He shoved me ahead of him, so I almost plowed into her. She grabbed my hand and started pumping it up and down. "Sure, I know Davey. He's a fine boy. . . a fine boy."

She had this funny smile on her face, and she was looking right over my head at Uncle Will. My arm was about to come unhinged at the elbow.

Uncle Will clapped his hands down on my shoulders. "Well, we'd better get going. Davey, tell your mother I'm sorry to miss out on her dinner, but I'll be home later."

I could just imagine how sorry he was to be missing Mom's dinner. The lucky stiff was probably on his way to Burger King. Not a zucchini dish on the whole menu.

"Okay, I'll tell her, Uncle Will," I said, slipping out of Mrs. Guptill's iron grip. I figured she must work out with weights, or at least an E-Z Pump-Up Muscle Builder. Nobody could develop hands like that just from driving a school bus.

Uncle Will followed Mrs. Guptill to the bus. They were so busy talking, they didn't notice Brad shooting baskets in the driveway. Brad noticed them, though. He stood there with his mouth hanging open and almost got beaned by the ball as it bounced off the rim.

"Where the heck is Uncle Will going with the Water Buffalo?"

"To the movies."

"You're kidding. On a date?"

"Of course not." Geez! Brad was always making such a big deal out of everything.

Uncle Will and Mrs. Guptill had climbed into the bus, and she gunned it out of the driveway. Uncle Will grinned and waved.

I waved back, but Brad just shook his head. "What a pair they make," he snickered. "Loony and the Beast."

Chapter 8

Uncle Will went over to Mrs. Guptill's house for dinner a couple of times in the next few weeks. I hated Mom's zucchini dishes, but not enough to go to the Water Buffalo's to eat. I figured Uncle Will must be really desperate. He was starting to seem happier, though, and he'd been acting pretty normal. That's why, when Brad's basketball banquet came up, Mom thought it would be okay to leave Uncle Will and me home alone together.

"I made a casserole for you two. It's in the refrigerator. Just put it in the microwave on reheat for ten minutes." She was leaning over the kitchen table, trying to put on nail polish while she talked.

"Okay, Mom. We'll be fine," I said.

"I'm sure you will, Davey. I wouldn't leave you if I had any doubts."

Dad stuck his head in the back door. "Can we move things along a little faster, Janet? Brad's coach said he wanted him there on time."

"I'm doing my best, John. I just have two more nails to go."

"I can't figure out why you always leave the nail polish until the last second."

"It's very simple, John. Once you have wet polish on your nails, you can't do anything else. It has to be last." Dad rolled his eyes and held the door for her. She started out, waving both hands in the air to dry the nail polish. Then she stopped and turned around. "Look, Davey, if you feel uneasy about this . . . about being alone with Uncle Will . . ."

"Aw, Mom. Get going, will you? We'll be fine."

After they left, I heated up the casserole, then dished up two plates and called Uncle Will to dinner.

"What's the name of this one?" he asked, holding some of it up on his fork to see it better.

"I don't know. At least it isn't green. I don't think she used any zucchini this time."

Uncle Will took a bite. "Mmph! Guess again," he said, shoving his plate away and gulping half a glass of milk.

I tasted it. It had tomatoes and even some meat in it, but most of it was zucchini. To top it off, Mom had used some real hot spice. "This is the worst one yet," I said.

Uncle Will went to the cupboard and pulled out two bowls and a box of Cheerios. "I believe you're right, Davey," he said, sliding a bowl across the table to me.

We ate our cereal in silence; then Uncle Will excused himself and went into the living room. I scraped our plates into Kaiser's bowl. The dog trotted right over, wolfed it all down, then looked at me as if I'd just given him a dish of rat poison. He galloped into the bathroom and slurped water from the toilet bowl for about five minutes straight. I nudged Kaiser out of the way and dumped the rest of the casserole down the toilet. It took three flushes to get rid of all the evidence. Kaiser wouldn't drink any more water out of the toilet after that.

I stacked up the dishes in the sink, wiped up the table with a sponge, and went into the living room. The TV was on, but Uncle Will had already fallen asleep in his chair. I watched a "M*A*S*H" rerun and a game show while I did my math homework. Uncle Will snored softly in the background. Then there was a real loud commercial for Crazy Louie's Used Car Lot that woke him up. He didn't say anything, just got up and stood for the longest time looking out the back window with his hands in his pockets.

"Full moon," he said, finally. "Perfect night for a murder."

"Yeah," I mumbled, not paying much attention.

A few minutes later, I could hear him digging around in the kitchen drawer, so I went to see what he was after. I got there just in time to see him pull Mom's butcher knife out of the drawer.

"Uncle Will? What are you doing?"

"Nothing, boy. Go back to your television."

He went out the back door. I was right behind him. "Wait, Uncle Will!" I had to think of something to stop him. "How about a game of checkers or something?" Not great, but it was all I could think of.

He kept going past the barn. I had to trot along beside him to keep up. The moon was so bright, the trees were casting shadows.

"Maybe later," he said. "Right now there's something I have to take care of. Go on back to the house. No sense you getting mixed up in this."

"No!" I shouted. Then, remembering I was supposed to humor him, I added, "Listen, Uncle Will, there's a great show that's just starting on television. Why don't you come watch it with me? Then you can come out later and do . . . uh . . . whatever it was you wanted to do."

"Nope. I've put it off too long already. Besides, the moon is perfect right now."

"Perfect for what?" I asked, dreading the answer.

"I told you before," he said. "Murder."

"You mean you're going to kill the chickens?"

Uncle Will laughed. "Nope. The only ones who kill chickens by moonlight are foxes and skunks." I could see the long blade glinting in the moonlight. Geez! Now what was I supposed to do? I didn't dare run back and try to call Mom and Dad. No telling how far Uncle Will could get while I was gone, and we'd never find him in the dark.

"I suppose now that you've tagged along, you might as well help," he said. "Can you keep your mouth shut afterward?"

"Help?" I squeaked. "Me?"

His teeth and the whites of his eyes seemed to glow in the purple light, and I could see twin reflections of the moon in his glasses. Now I knew the meaning of the word *lunatic*.

He put his hand on my shoulder. "Yep. You're my partner in crime now, whether you want to be or not. Here, take this." He shoved something cold and metallic into my hand. I looked down at it. It was a big long-handled spoon.

"What am I supposed to do with this?" I whispered.

"After I carve them up," he said, "you can scoop out their insides."

I could feel my Cheerios lurching back up toward my throat. That did it. Mom had been wrong. There was no humoring Uncle Will or stopping him. All I could do now was run for my life, call the police, and just hope they got here before Uncle Will found somebody to carve up. I started to turn away, but he grabbed my arm and said, "Here's a likely prospect for my first victim." My heart stopped beating.

He let go of me and dropped to his knees. Then he raised the knife in the air and plunged it into something on the ground. It made a horrible juicy thunk, like the sound of a blade going through living guts. He stabbed it again and again. There wasn't enough light to see what he had, but whatever it was, it was dying a horrible death. I wanted to turn and run, but my feet stuck to the ground, like in one of those nightmares where a monster is coming at you, but you can't move.

Then he stood up and turned toward me, wiping the knife blade on his pants. I couldn't see the blood, but I knew there must be a lot of it. "Got a little carried away with that one," he said, with a wicked grin. "The rest we'll knock off the right way, slow and easy."

"The rest?" I asked, my voice cracking.

"Sure. You don't think we're stopping with one, do you?" He bent down again, lifted something out of a tangle of vines, and held it out to me. I'd have known that dark oval shape anywhere. It was still attached to the vine.

"A zucchini?" I said. "You're going to murder a zucchini?"

"Sure," he said, grinning. "Wha'd you think? I'm going to run around slicing up the neighbors?"

"I didn't . . . I thought . . . I just . . ." I couldn't seem to finish a sentence.

He tilted the unattached end of the zucchini toward the moonlight and cut a small circle out of it. Then he held it out to me. "Here, quit your babbling and scoop the insides out to about halfway down. And be careful you don't pull it loose from the vine."

"But why? When Mom finds out we did this, she's going to murd . . . uh . . . be real mad at us."

"Not if you keep your mouth shut, she won't. Now, get busy, we have about a hundred more of these things to go."

I didn't ask any more questions. I just worked along next to him, scooping out the insides of the squash and hiding the pulp under the leafy vines. Our eyes had adjusted to the blue light, so it was almost like working in daylight. I was so glad that the murder victims were zucchinis instead of people, I didn't even worry about what would happen when Mom found out.

I stayed away from Mom as long as I could the next day after school, but when she called us all to the dinner table, I didn't have any choice. I went into the kitchen and slid into my seat.

Brad came in right after me. "Wow, dinner smells good, for a change," he said. "What is it?"

"Meat loaf," Mom answered, setting the brown crusty loaf on the table.

"You got zucchinis in there?" Brad asked.

He poked at the meat loaf a few times with his fork before Mom slapped his hand away. "No, I'm afraid there was an attack on our garden last night and the zucchini were all ruined."

Brad let out a whoop. "All right! Who got 'em? Our Fairy Godmother?"

Mom pretended not to hear him, but her eyebrow went up. "Uncle Will says it looks like the work of the squash ferret. They just eat a hole in the blossom end and scoop out about half of the insides, so they can get at the seeds."

I choked and put my head down, sneaking a look out of the corner of my eye at Uncle Will. He looked at me and I saw his right eyebrow go up, just like Mom's. I looked away and bit my bottom lip.

"The squash ferret?" Dad said. "I don't believe I've ever heard of that animal."

Uncle Will looked him right in the eye. "They're pretty rare in these parts," he said evenly. "Most people never heard of them."

"I see," Dad said, spreading his napkin on his lap. He turned to me. "They ever say anything in school about squash ferrets, Davey?"

"Yeah, I remember hearing something about them, probably in science class," I said. "I think they're native to Canada. That's why you don't see many around here."

"Only the hardy few that manage to swim across Lake Ontario, I presume," Dad said. He looked back and forth between me and Uncle Will, then shook his head and smiled.

Brad sawed off a huge hunk of meat loaf for himself. "Well, I don't care if nobody in the whole world ever heard of them. I'm going to buy a giant bag of Purina Squash Ferret Chow to keep that thing alive until next summer. It saved our lives."

Mom put a dish of mashed potatoes on the table and sat down. "I must say, I'm almost relieved that the zucchini are gone," she said. "I didn't have the heart to waste them, but it was hard to think of different ways to use them every day."

"You were very creative, Jan," Dad said. "I'd even have to say extremely creative."

Mom smiled.

We had a wonderful dinner that night—meat loaf, mashed potatoes and gravy, green beans, and, for dessert, vanilla pudding with orange slices. Uncle Will and I had three helpings each. Of everything!

Chapter 9

I decided Uncle Will wasn't crazy after all. Anybody who could figure out how to get rid of all those zucchinis was a genius as far as I was concerned. Mom's cooking was back to normal, too, except for a couple of loaves of bread she baked from the wheat we threshed and winnowed.

The bread looked okay on the outside and even smelled pretty good when it was baking, but each loaf weighed a ton, and the crust was so hard and tough you could've broken a tooth on it. Uncle Will said she didn't grind the flour fine enough, which was probably because she had to do it in the blender. Luckily, it was impossible to slice the bread without a chain saw, or Mom might have tried to make sandwiches out of it to put in my lunch.

Dad was still having a hard time getting used to living on a farm. Brad wasn't too wild about it either, but he got out of doing a lot of the chores because he was tied up with the basketball team most days after school. Dad usually cornered him on the weekends, though, especially when it was time to get the wood split for winter.

I heard them arguing out by the woodpile one Saturday morning.

"Aw, come on, Dad. It'll take me all morning to get through these logs. Why can't Davey do some of the work?"

"Splitting wood takes a lot of strength, Brad. Davey can help out when he's older, but for now, it's your responsibility. If you'd just stop complaining and start working, you'd have the job half finished by now."

Brad spotted me. "Yeah. Well, maybe if Davey tried doing some of the work around here, he'd develop some muscles. Then he wouldn't have to keep snitching my E-Z Pump-Up Muscle Builder when I'm not around."

How did he know about that? Did he have our room bugged?

Brad took a swing with the maul and got it hung up in a hunk of wood. "Here, let me have that," Dad said. He held the log down with his foot and wriggled the maul back and forth until it came loose. Brad took it and tried again. This time he hit the log off center and the maul bounced off, nearly hitting his foot.

"Geez, Dad. I'm going to kill myself trying to do this. Why can't we just heat with the gas furnace this winter like normal people?"

"I know what you mean, son, but your mother has her heart set on using that old wood stove in the living room, at least during the evenings. You know the scene—farm family gathers around the homestead hearth."

"So all of a sudden we move to the country and turn into the Waltons, right?"

"I guess that's about the way we look from your mother's point of view," Dad said. "Anyway, you'll get the hang of this with a little more practice. Just be careful, John Boy."

"Very funny," Brad muttered. "I'll probably end up cutting both my feet off."

"Then you'd be too short to play on the basketball team," Dad said, and went into the house.

"Davey, get over here and prop this thing up with your foot, will you?" Brad yelled.

"No way! I'm already too short."

"Thanks a bunch. Wait till you need a favor from me." Brad set the log up on end, but it fell over before he could take a swing.

"Got a problem there, Brad?" Uncle Will called from the barn, where he was feeding the chickens.

"Naw. It's okay, Uncle Will."

"Maybe he can help," I whispered.

"Are you kidding? The old coot couldn't even lift this thing, let alone split a log with it. I don't need him putting in his two cent's worth." Brad swung again. The log tipped over just before he hit it, and the maul was buried in its side.

By this time, Uncle Will had put away the chicken feed. He came over to where Brad was struggling with the maul. "Mind if I give you a few pointers?" he asked, taking the maul handle and jerking it loose.

"Sure. Fire away, Uncle Will." Brad turned toward me, so Uncle Will couldn't see him, and made his "loony" face.

"Well, first off, you can't choke up on the handle like that. You want to start off with your right hand up against the head of the maul. And there's a rhythm to it, with a little beat at the top of the swing. Just try the first part. Like this. Up and hold. Up and hold." Uncle Will swung the maul up over his shoulder a few times, then handed it to Brad.

Brad was getting impatient. "Look, Uncle Will. Thanks for your help and all, but I was doing okay. I think I'll just keep doing it the way—"

"You weren't doing okay, boy. You were about to split your fool skull in two. Now try it my way."

The tone of Uncle Will's voice surprised Brad. "Okay, okay. I'll try it. What was it? Up and hold, right?" Brad tried. Then Uncle Will repositioned his hands on the maul handle and he tried again.

"Now you're gettin' it. I'll show you how to carry through."

Uncle Will kicked two big logs over to us and lined them up to form a V. Then he stood a third one up against them so it was supported by the angle. "You gotta give the logs something to lean on. They're not just going to stand at attention waitin' for you to knock 'em silly."

I could tell that Brad didn't think Uncle Will had a prayer of splitting that log. As a matter of fact, neither did I.

"Now watch what I do with my right hand." Uncle Will swung the maul up over his head. There was that little pause again, then he brought the maul down. At the same time his right hand slid all the way down the handle to meet his other hand. There was a crack like a gunshot, as two pieces of the log flew in opposite directions.

Brad let out a whistle.

Uncle Will grinned. "Didn't think an old coot like me could split a log, did you?"

Brad looked embarrassed. "That was pretty good. How did you do it?"

"Two things you gotta remember, and you'll be fine. First, slide that right hand down nice and steady, and the maul will pick up speed. And the most important thing is to keep your eye dead-center on that log. Don't ever look at the maul. Here. Give 'er a try."

Brad took the maul from Uncle Will and slid his hand up and down the handle. "I don't know. Maybe I should watch one more time."

Uncle Will set up a new log. "Nonsense. I've seen you sink them baskets in your games at school. You've got the eye of a hawk, boy. Now use it."

Brad took a deep breath and stared at the log as if he had X-ray vision. When he raised the maul and brought it down, it went through the log like butter.

"All right!" Brad yelled. Uncle Will had set up another log, and Brad split it easily.

"This is a piece of cake," Brad said. "I'll have this pile split in no time. Thanks, Uncle Will."

"Your brother's a regular Paul Bunyan now, Davey. Next year we can take him along on our zucchini massacre and have the job done twice as fast." He winked at me and headed back to the barn.

Brad stopped and leaned on the maul. "What did he mean by that? Were you two the ones who got rid of the zucchinis?"

"Yeah, but you'd better not say anything to Mom. Not unless you want a whole summer of green meals again next year."

Brad shook his head. "I thought there was something fishy about that squash ferret business. Maybe the old guy isn't so bad after all."

Score one for Uncle Will.

School was going along pretty well now. I was getting to know some of the kids, but the only one who lived near me was Sara Weiderman. That's why Sara and I got assigned as partners to work on a project for the Science Fair.

We had decided to build a volcano out of papier-mâché, with lava made from baking soda and vinegar, an idea we got from Sara's *Experiments at Home* book. We built the volcano in Sara's barn. Then, when it dried, we planned to decorate it at my house, so we could use Mom's acrylics to paint it.

Sara still didn't talk much, but she was okay to work with. She was the one who came up with the idea of gathering up the last layer of newspaper into folds, to make jagged little channels for the lava to run down.

"We only have two more days until the deadline. You think we can get the volcano all painted this afternoon?" I asked her on the school bus.

"Sure," she said, staring straight ahead.

As we went by our house, Uncle Will was standing out in the driveway. He waved at the bus, and I waved back. So did Mrs. Guptill, with a goofy-looking smile on her face. When Sara and I got up by the front door, Mrs. Guptill said, "How's your uncle Will doing, Davey?"

Why was she asking about him? He'd just been over at her house two nights ago.

Mrs. Guptill blew a strand of hair out of her eyes as she rounded the corner onto Berg Road. "Did ya hear me, Davey? I was asking after your uncle Will."

"Oh, yeah. He's fine, Mrs. Guptill. He's been real busy helping us get settled into the farm. He used to be a farmer, you know. Had his own farm and everything. A big one." There. That ought to let the old busybody know Uncle Will wasn't just some loony who was looking for a good meal. Mrs. Guptill had picked up a little too much speed talking to me, so she had to jam on the brakes when we got to Sara's driveway. I was thrown into the door-opening bar, then bounced back and almost landed in Dora Simpson's lap. Mrs. Guptill always caught me off guard with her sudden stops. Sara must have been used to her. She just planted both feet on the floor and never even tilted.

We got off and ran out to Sara's barn to get the volcano. It looked really good, worth the three school nights we'd spent on it so far. We had started by nailing a chicken-wire base to a big board, and built up a few layers of the wet paper each night. Even with the newspaper print all over it, and an ad for Andy's Appliance Outlet Fall Closeout Sale plastered over the south slope, you could imagine it was a real volcano.

"The thing looks great, Sara. When we get it painted and have the lava run out of it, I bet it'll win a blue ribbon."

"It's all right," Sara said.

We left our books in Sara's barn and started out through the woods. I took the lead, holding the board behind me, and Sara followed, hanging on to the other end. I was busy watching where I stepped so I wouldn't trip on a rock and mash our mountain, when all of a sudden I was looking at an extra pair of sneakers. Two extra pairs of sneakers. And all four feet were attached to long, skinny legs.

"Hey, Leo," Lester said. "Ain't this here a pretty sight? Davey and his little girlfriend have been doing an art project."

"Yeah," Leo chimed in. "What is that thing? A vase to put little flowers in, Davey boy?"

"You jerks just get out of the way and leave us alone," Sara growled. "Keep going, Davey." She shoved me ahead by butting me in the rear with the volcano. At the same time, Leo stuck his foot out to trip me and, as I fell, Lester wrestled the volcano away from Sara.

"You big, stupid creep!" Sara yelled. "Put that down or you'll be sorry."

As soon as I hit the ground, Leo jerked me up by the back of my jacket and shoved me against a big tree. Lester dropped the volcano and dragged Sara over next to me. Then he picked up a big looped-up clothesline from where he had it hidden behind a bush and threw one end to Leo. Before we knew what was happening, the Spiders were running in opposite directions around the tree, winding the rope around us, as if we were two flies being spun up into a web.

"You guys are going to be sorry you ever messed

with Davey Anderson," Sara yelled, struggling against the ropes.

The Spiders met in front of us and stopped, grinning, each pulling hard on his end of the rope. Lester laughed. "I'm scared to death, ain't you, Leo? What do ya think that mean old Davey Anderson'll do to us?"

"He's going to smash you to smithereens," Sara screamed. "He's going to beat you to a bloody pulp. He's going to—" I finally managed to kick Sara in the ankle. My foot was about the only thing I could still move.

"Knock it off, will you, Sara?" I whispered.

There was no stopping Sara. She probably hadn't said more than twenty-five words to me the whole time I'd known her, and now I couldn't shut her up. The Spiders were circling the tree again, winding up the last of the rope.

"Davey Anderson has a black belt in karate," Sara shouted. "His hands and feet are registered with the FBI as lethal weapons."

"Sara," I hissed. "You're signing my death sentence here."

The mouth kept going. "Davey Anderson has more strength in the little finger of his left hand than you two idiots have in your whole entire bodies."

I could feel the rope yank tighter as the Spiders knotted the ends behind the tree. Then they ran around in front, and Lester picked up the volcano again. "I'm so scared, Leo, ain't you?"

"Yeah," Leo piped in a squeaky little voice. "I'm so blinkin' scared I'm going to climb up a tree to get away from that mean old Davey Anderson. And I'll use this here footstool to give me a boost."

Leo grabbed the volcano away from his brother and set it down at the base of a nearby tree, then stepped on the crater at the top. As he put his full weight on it, our beautiful mountain started to crumple. Now the south slope read, "Andy's Apple Fallout Sale."

"This footstool don't seem to be working right, Lester. You try it."

"Geronimo!" yelled Lester as he sailed through the air, landing on the volcano with both big feet. Now there was nothing left but a papier-mâché accordion on a wooden base.

The Spiders turned and walked over to us, grinning. Luckily, Sara was so mad she couldn't say anything. She was breathing hard, though—so hard I could feel the rope tighten every time she inhaled.

"That was a crummy footstool you guys made." Leo laughed. "C'mon, Lester. All this running around made me hungry. Let's go home and make hot fudge sundaes."

Lester nodded his shaggy head. "Yeah, with whipped cream and nuts. And maybe a bag of potato chips, a couple of candy bars, and some pop to wash it all down. Too bad you two can't join us. I guess you're tied up, huh?" The Spiders slapped each other on the back and laughed at Lester's dumb joke.

Sara regained her powers of speech. "No wonder you two are so stupid," she yelled. "You've burned out your brains with junk food. When Davey Anderson gets loose from this tree, he's going to make you pay for this."

Leo put his hands around my throat, just tight enough so that when I tried to swallow I could feel his thumbs pressing on my Adam's apple. "So what are you going to do to us, Davey boy? I'm all ears."

Sara spoke up. "He's going to make you wish you had never been born. He's going to—" I kicked her again.

Leo tightened his grip on my neck. "I asked Davey. Not you, motor mouth."

Just then I heard a low growling sound coming from Sara's direction. She was really going off the deep end now. No telling what she would say next.

The growling got louder, and I realized it wasn't coming from Sara after all. The Spiders heard it, too. "Geez! What was that?" Leo asked, turning to look at Lester, who was standing in front of a thick section of bushes.

The noises got louder, with snarls and snorts. "Cut it out, Lester," Leo whined, letting go of my throat. "That ain't funny. You know I hate big dogs."

The bushes started to quiver. Lester ran over to his brother. "I wasn't doing nothing, Leo. There's something big in that bush, and it ain't no dog." The two of them started backing away from the bush, clinging to each other.

"Sara," I whispered. "We've got to get loose. Can you get a hand free?"

We both struggled against the ropes. "I can't move," she said. "It's wound around too tight."

"Well, try harder. Whatever's in that bush sounds big and mad. We're sitting ducks here."

There was a sudden roar and the bushes shook

violently. The thing in the bush was coming out. The Spiders fell all over each other trying to escape.

"Outa my way," Lester yelled, pushing Leo.

"Me first. Stop shoving."

They disappeared down the path in a tangle of spidery arms and legs, still yelling and pounding on each other.

The snorting, snarling, and growling grew louder and bushes parted. We were face to face with the monster. It was Uncle Will.

He came running over to us. "I did good, Ray, huh? Didn't I? I saved you from them big mean boys, didn't I? Huh?" Uncle Will had that little kid expression on his face, and he was jiggling from one foot to the other with excitement.

Sara's eyes were wide. "Who is this guy?" she whispered. "Do you know him?" I guess she'd never noticed him standing in our driveway when we went by in the bus.

"Yeah. He's my great-uncle," I said. I turned to Uncle Will. "You did just fine, Willie. Now can you untie us? The knots are in the back of the tree."

Uncle Will scowled and stuck out his bottom lip. "What do I get if I do? Will you let me play stickball with you and the older kids?"

"Sure, Willie."

Uncle Will's face brightened. "And—and—and will you take me in to the soda fountain for a phosphate?"

"Yeah, Willie. It's a deal. Just untie us, okay?"

Uncle Will went around behind the tree, and we could feel him yanking on the rope.

"What's with him?" Sara whispered. "Is he retarded?"

"No. He isn't like this all the time. Just once in a while he gets confused and thinks he's a little kid again and I'm his older brother. Then pretty soon he's okay. He's kind of weird, but I don't think he's really crazy."

"Sounds to me like he's just senile. A lot of old people get that way. My grandmother didn't know who she was half the time."

Uncle Will came back around the tree, looking about ready to cry. "I forgot, Ray," he said.

"What's the matter, Willie?" I asked. "What did you forget?"

"I forgot I don't know how to untie knots if they're double. These are more than double. These are threeple or fourple. Does—does this mean I won't get the phosphate?" he asked, his lower lip starting to tremble.

"No, wait a minute," I said. "I'll think of something."

"Do you have a jackknife, Davey?" Sara whispered. "Maybe he could cut us free."

"I don't, but I bet he does. He whittles a lot. . . . Hey, Willie. Look in your pockets and see if you have a jackknife."

Uncle Will looked surprised. "Ma don't let me carry no knife, Ray. You know that."

"Yeah, Willie, I know. But maybe one got in there by mistake. Just check, okay?"

Uncle Will started to feel around in the pockets of his overalls. He pulled out a wadded-up Kleenex and turned it over and over in his hands as if he'd never seen anything like it before.

"I don't think they had Kleenex when he was a kid," Sara whispered.

"Yeah, you're probably right," I said. "Willie, never mind that. Keep looking for a knife."

Uncle Will plunged his hand deep into another pocket and pulled out his jackknife. He stared at it in disbelief, then held it out to me, his hand shaking. "Don't tell Ma, Ray. I didn't put this here knife in my pocket, honest. Please don't tell Ma and Pa." There were tears in his eyes.

"Don't worry, Willie. The knife just got in there by mistake. I won't tell anybody anything."

Uncle Will grinned, wiping his nose on his sleeve. "Thanks, Ray. You're a good big brother."

"You, too, Willie," I said. "You're one terrific little brother. Now just cut us loose so we can go home."

Uncle Will opened the knife and started hacking away at the rope near my wrist. "It don't work right, Ray. It won't cut through the rope."

"Let me see the knife, Willie," Sara said. "There, that's the problem. You're using the wrong edge of the blade. Turn it over."

"Like this?"

"That's it. Why don't you move a little farther away from Ray's wrist so you don't cut him."

Uncle Will scowled. "I wouldn't cut my brother. Who is she anyway, Ray?"

"Sara is a friend of mine, Willie. She's in my class at school."

Uncle Will peered closely at Sara. "She's pretty. She your girlfriend?"

Sara giggled. "No, nothing like that, Willie. Your brother and I are just friends. Keep working on the rope, okay?"

Willie sawed away at the rope. His hands were clumsy, which seemed strange because he always handled the knife like an expert when he whittled. "Watch it, Willie. You're going to cut off a finger if you're not careful," I said.

"Am not! I ain't even close to your fingers, Ray."

"I'm talking about your fingers, not mine."

"Oh. Well, it don't matter anyway. I'm through." He took one last tug at the rope, and the two pieces he had been working on fell to the ground, freeing our hands. We all pulled at the rest of the rope to loosen it, and Sara and I were free.

"Thanks, Willie," Sara said, rubbing her arm. You could still see the marks left by the rope. "You saved our lives."

Uncle Will ducked his head and kicked at some stones in the path.

"Yeah, that was great, Willie," I said. "Why don't you let me have the knife now, and we'll all go back to the house."

Uncle Will handed me the knife. I figured I could get it back to him later when he was himself again.

Sara and I picked up the ruined volcano, and we all started down the path for home. Uncle Will was way ahead of us.

"I like Willie," Sara said.

"Yeah, me too. He kind of grows on you. Uncle

Will is pretty nice when he's being himself too. It's like having two friends instead of one." I realized that sounded kind of dumb, so I added, "At least he keeps things from getting boring."

Sara laughed. "Yes, I can believe that."

Uncle Will stopped and turned around. "I know something you two don't know."

"What's that, Willie?" Sara called back to him.

"I got me a girlfriend too," he said, grinning.

"Listen Willie, Sara's not my girl—"

"Oh, knock it off, Davey," Sara interrupted. "Who is she, Willie? Do we know your girlfriend?"

"Maybe you do and maybe you don't," he said. He turned and went on down the path ahead of us, chuckling to himself. He was really off his rocker today. Where would he find a girlfriend? The only two women he'd seen, since he moved in with us, were Mom and the Water Buffalo.

Chapter 10

Uncle Will was halfway up the back meadow by the time we reached the bridge. He seemed to have forgotten about us and hadn't turned around for a while. Sara and I couldn't walk very fast carrying the volcano, so by the time we got up to the house, Uncle Will was already sitting at the kitchen table.

Mom was standing behind him. She had a real funny look on her face. "Davey, I'm glad you're here. Uncle Will isn't feeling . . . quite himself." Her hands were flitting around like mad.

Uncle Will looked up, grinning. "Hi, Ray. Hi, Ray's girlfriend."

"I'm Sara, Willie, remember?" We set the volcano down on the table, and Sara slid into the seat next to Uncle Will.

"Girlfriend?" Mom asked, looking at me.

"This is Sara Weiderman, Mom. She's the one I was assigned to do this science project with. She lives over on Berg Road."

"Oh. Nice to meet you, Sara. You seem to have met Uncle Will."

"Yeah," Uncle Will chimed in. "Ray and his

girlfriend were out in the woods tied up to a tree, and these big mean guys were doing bad things to them, and I jumped out of a bush and saved them."

Geez! He was blabbing the whole thing about the Spiders to Mom. Before I could think of something to say, Mom patted him on the shoulder and said, "That's nice, Uncle Will. I'm sure you must be very tired after all that excitement. Why don't I fix us all some hot chocolate, and then you can take a nap for a little while." That was a close call. I guess she figured it was such a wild story it couldn't be true.

Uncle Will pushed himself away from the table. "I don't take naps no more. You can't make me neither." He stomped off to his room. Mom stood there with her mouth hanging open for a minute, then followed him. I sat down next to Sara, and we stared in silence at what was left of our volcano.

"We're going to get even with those Spiders," Sara finally muttered, picking at a broken piece of papier-mâché.

"Never mind about the Spiders, Sara. It's the volcano we have to worry about. We have to fix it up before tomorrow night."

"Fix *what* up? In case you haven't noticed, Davey, our mountain has turned into a plateau. A very short plateau."

"Maybe we can stretch it back up or something."

"Oh, sure."

"No, really. It might work. Grab the other side of the crater," I said. "Let's see if we can raise it back up again."

"It's not going to work, Davey," Sara insisted,

but she took hold of her side, and we pulled together. It was no use. No matter how carefully we tried to lift and reshape the mountain, pieces of dried papier-mâché kept cracking and falling off. Pretty soon we had a chicken-wire mountain with a confetti base.

"See? I told you it wouldn't work," Sara said, slumping down in her chair. "We're right back to where we started, and there isn't any time to redo the papier-mâché and get it to dry."

"There must be some way to speed up the drying," I said, thinking out loud. "How about a hair dryer. . . or maybe the oven?"

"Oh, brilliant, Davey. You're going to bake paper in the oven? Then we can have a living model of a forest fire."

Mom came back into the room.

"Is Uncle Will okay now, Mom?" I asked.

"He's stretched out on his bed, and I think he's almost asleep. He didn't seem to know who I was."

"He'll come out of it, Mom. He did before. You heard him call me Ray. He thought I was his brother."

"And he thought I was your girlfriend," Sara said, giggling.

"Yeah, well that just shows how messed up in the head he is."

"Davey!" Mom said. "That's no way to talk about Uncle Will, or to treat a guest. . . . How is your science project coming along?"

"That's it!" I said, pointing to the mess on the table.

"It was supposed to be a papier-mâché volcano," Sara explained. "But it got broken when—" I shot her a look. "When something fell on it in my barn."

"That's a shame," Mom said. "Is there time to rebuild it?"

"I don't think so, Mom. That paper junk takes too long to dry. The Science Fair is tomorrow night. You're looking at an automatic F for both of us."

"Maybe all is not lost," Mom said. "I used to make a kind of clay for craft projects out of bread. It usually dries overnight, but you can bake it in the oven to speed things up a bit."

"No kidding, Mom. Bread? How do you do it?"

"As I recall, we used to crumble a loaf of bread up in a bowl and mix it with just enough white glue to make it feel like clay." She went over to the bread box. "Well, we don't have the right kind of bread. It's supposed to be the cheap white stuff from the supermarket. All I have here is the bread I baked."

"Gee, Mom. That would be perfect to make a mountain out of. It would make a neat rock effect."

Mom raised her eyebrow.

"I didn't mean the bread was like a rock, Mom. I just meant the whole wheat flour would look more like rocks than the white stuff."

"Never mind, Davey. I know what you meant. The family hasn't exactly been devouring my efforts in the bread-baking department." She held up the bread, turning it in her hands to admire it. "I guess I could sacrifice this last loaf for a good cause. Besides, it's getting stale."

Stale? How could she tell?

"You have to crumble it up in a big bowl, then add about one teaspoon of glue for each slice of bread. Knead it with your hands until it feels like clay. Then take pieces of it and roll them out on waxed paper to make thin sheets. You should be able to press those onto your wire frame."

"Okay, Mom. Thanks. Come on, Sara. I'll start with the bread, and you can pull the chicken wire off the board and pick the rest of the paper off it. We'll need a base to shape the mountain, like before."

"Well, I'll leave you two to your project," Mom said. "I'll be out in the barn if you need me. When you get to the baking, put it in for about an hour at three hundred and fifty degrees. That should do it, as long as you haven't made the clay too thick."

I put the bread in a big mixing bowl and tried to crumble it. I hacked at it with a fork for a few minutes but didn't make a dent.

Sara watched over my shoulder. "That's some loaf of bread," she said. "Does your mother bake much?"

"Very funny," I said. "Skip the wisecracks and come up with a way to make this rock into bread crumbs."

"Hi, Davey. Have a friend over today?" Dad was home from work. I introduced Sara to him and explained our problem.

"I know your mother's bread was a bit tough, Davey, but surely it isn't indestructible. Let me try it." He got a good grip on the loaf with both hands and tried to rip off a hunk, but nothing happened.

"Let me have that fork, Davey."

"I'm telling you, Dad. This bread is made of steel."

"Nonsense. You just need to apply a little more force than . . . oops."

The fork broke in half, but there still wasn't a

dent in the bread. "This calls for heavier artillery," Dad said. He went out into the garage and came back with a chisel and a big wooden mallet.

He put the bread on the bread board and positioned the chisel right in the middle of the loaf. "Stand back, you two. I don't want anybody to be hit by flying shrapnel." He pounded the chisel a couple of times, but nothing happened.

"Maybe we should take it out to the woodpile and split it with the maul," I said.

"I'm saving that as a last resort." Dad whacked at it a few more times, and the bread finally split in half.

"Hey, that's great, Dad. Thanks."

"You and Sara can finish this up. I have to go call the Highway Department."

"Really, Dad? Why do you have to call the Highway Department?"

"I want to see if I can interest them in buying your mother's bread recipe. If they used this stuff instead of concrete, the roads would last a lifetime."

"Your dad's funny," Sara said after Dad left the room.

"Yeah, I know. He's always making jokes without cracking a smile. I'm the only one in the family who ever picks up on what he's doing and hands him straight lines. If Mom or Brad had been here he would've kept saying he was going to call the Highway Department over and over, until somebody asked him why."

"If your mom had been here, I don't think he would have made a joke about her recipe in the first place," Sara said, walloping the daylights out of the bread.

Sara and I spent the next half hour taking turns trying to pound the bread into crumbs. Then we added the glue, and after another half hour the mess started to feel like clay.

Sara had reshaped the chicken wire and put it on a cookie sheet. Then, working from both sides, we rolled out little sheets of clay and pressed them into the wire. At first, hunks of the clay squeezed right through the wire, but then we started getting the hang of it.

As Sara and I worked along quietly, we heard a rattling sound coming from under the sink.

"What the heck was that?" I asked.

"Just sounds like a mouse," Sara said, without looking up. "Everybody who doesn't own a cat around here has mice in the house."

"Wait till Mom hears about that. We'll probably have to keep mice as pets, too."

"Your mother likes mice?"

"Not particularly, but she has this thing about not killing animals. She had a bad experience with a chicken."

We kept turning the wire frame as we worked, ending up with just enough bread clay to cover it.

Sara sat back and admired our volcano. "I don't believe it," Sara said when the wire was covered. "I think it's going to work."

Sara started pinching little jagged channels down the sides of the mountain while I turned on the oven and set the timer. We had to take a rack out of the oven so the top of the mountain would fit.

While we waited for our masterpiece to bake, I got out the poster boards and markers we'd bought to make signs to go with our exhibit. Sara did the drawing of the cross section of a volcano, because she was a much better artist than me. I had tried sketching it in my science notebook, but mine looked like the cross section of a zit in the Clearasil commercials.

After the bread had been baking about fifteen minutes, Brad came bursting into the kitchen. "Something smells great," he said. "What's Mom baking?"

"She's not baking," I said. "We are."

Brad opened the over door. "What the heck is this thing?"

"A mountain," Sara answered.

Brad slammed the oven door and stormed out of the kitchen. "Just once!" he yelled over his shoulder. "Just once, I'd like to have some normal food around this place."

When the timer finally went off, we put on potholder mitts and pulled the volcano out of the oven. It was tricky to handle because it was heavy and started sliding around on the cookie sheet, but we managed to get it over to the table.

"It looks good, Davey," Sara said, standing back and squinting at the volcano. "Much better than the first one. I don't think we even need to paint it."

She was right. The mountain was golden brown, shading to darker streaks here and there. It looked a lot more natural than it would have if we just painted it solid brown. I tapped the side of the volcano with a fork. It made a sharp pinging sound like a ceramic bowl.

"This is terrific," I said. "The crust came out even harder than it did when it was baked the first time."

"Okay," Sara said. "Let's try the lava to see how it's going to look." She put a couple of tablespoons of baking soda into the crater. Then I poured the vinegar on top, just as Brad came back through the kitchen. The mixture bubbled and sputtered, then erupted over the top of the crater and ran down the channels Sara had modeled in the dough.

"Don't look now," Brad said, "but your mountain just threw up."

Chapter 11

The whole family went to the Science Fair the next night, except for Brad, of course. It was raining a little bit when we started out, so I put some plastic wrap over the volcano. I wasn't about to mess up our chances of getting a blue ribbon now.

Sara arrived at school at the same time we did. The whole gym was filled with tables, and kids were setting up their displays.

We passed six or seven models of the solar system. One kid must have thought up his project at the last minute, because all he had were nine old golf balls with the names of the planets scrawled on them and a grapefruit labeled "Son." He was trying to get them lined up in order, but the table was kind of slanted, so the grapefruit kept rolling right past Pluto and on into oblivion. Uncle Will stopped off to look at a project with baby chicks hatching in a homemade incubator.

Sara and I finally found the table with our name on it. We set up the posters on each side and the volcano in the middle. Dora Simpson had her display at the next able. She had a mother cat and a litter of kittens in a cardboard box with a big sign that said "Determining the Bloodlines of the Domestic Feline."

"What's that stupid thing supposed to be?" Dora asked, looking down her nose at our wrapped-up volcano.

I was just starting to take off the plastic wrap, but Sara stopped me. "Leave it covered up until the judges come around," she whispered. "I don't want that stupid Dora to see it."

I wandered casually over to Dora's display. "What's so great about this?" I asked. "A bunch of cats isn't much of a science project."

Dora gave me a smug little smile, her nose in the air. "I'm saving my scientific research for the judges. I have real proof of my facts. Photographs!"

"Big deal," Sara snapped. "Come on, Davey. Let's look at the other stuff."

Uncle Will was still talking to the kids who had hatched the baby chicks. They seemed really interested in what he was saying. I just hoped he wouldn't get into that business about sticking your fingers up a hen's rear to see if she's laying or not.

One kid had a cardboard maze with four gerbils in it. Each one had a little numbered collar. He leaned forward as we started to pass him and whispered, "Care to engage in a little sporting wager?"

Sara shook her head. "No thanks, Harold." She turned to me. "Watch out for this guy. He's the class con man."

Harold clutched his chest. "You have hurt me to the very depths of my being, Sara Weiderman. I was merely offering you a bit of diversion in this otherwise mundane display of unimaginative scientific trivia."

"Yeah?" Sara challenged. "Like what?"

Harold grinned. "For the paltry sum of twenty-five cents, you may choose a rodent to race through the maze against my trained gerbil, Sludge."

"What do we get if our gerbil wins?" I asked.

"I would refund your quarter and pay you an additional twenty-five cents, of course. This operation is absolutely honest and above board." Across the room, I noticed Mrs. Guptill talking with Uncle Will at the chick-hatching display. They were both grinning like fools, and she was sort of batting her eyelashes at him. I couldn't see why he needed to butter her up anymore. We were getting great meals at home, now that the zucchinis were gone.

"How about it?" Harold persisted. "Do you want to race or not?"

"Which one is Sludge?" I asked.

Harold pointed at an ordinary-looking gerbil. "That one—number one."

"He doesn't look any smarter than the rest, Sara," I said. "Let's give it a shot."

Sara rolled her eyes. "It's your quarter."

I fished the money out of my pocket. "Okay, Harold. You're on." I looked at the group of gerbils and picked out the one that seemed to have the most nervous energy.

"An admirable choice," Harold said. "That's Einstein."

Harold removed the other gerbils and lined Sludge and Einstein up at the starting gate. Then he sat down and leaned close to the maze. "On your mark, get set, go!" he said, releasing the two gerbils. Einstein turned around immediately and bumped into the wall behind the starting gate. Then he proceeded to try to chew a hole through it. Sludge, on the other hand, was making steady progress through the maze, without a single false turn.

"Come on, Einstein," I pleaded. "Turn around, will you?"

"I never saw a gerbil run that way, Harold," Sara said. "Why is he holding his head down so far?" She leaned close to the course and squinted at Sludge. "Something's fishy here."

"Don't be a poor loser," Harold replied, never taking his eyes off Sludge.

"You're cheating, Harold. I know you are." Sara put her face directly in front of Sludge and yelled, "Boo!"

Sludge stopped running. At least his feet stopped running. But Sludge was still moving steadily through the course, sliding on all four feet. Sara dove under the table. "Aha!" she yelled, wrestling something out of Harold's hand. She surfaced again with a huge magnet. When she held it just above Sludge, his collar jumped up and attached itself to the magnet with a loud clink, making Sludge stand up on his hind legs.

"Cute, Harold. I suppose he tap-dances, too," Sara said. She held out her hand until Harold reluctantly gave her back my quarter.

"Come on, Davey," she said. "The judges are almost to our table." She gave me my quarter without even saying "I told you so."

We hurried back and slid behind our display just as the judges reached Dora Simpson's table. Miss Hopewell, a fourth-grade teacher and one of the judges, was oohing and ahhing over the kittens. She was wearing a flowered dress that reminded me of the slipcover Mom made for our living room sofa. Miss Hopewell was also built a lot like our living room sofa.

The other judge was Mr. Cronmuller, the Science Editor from the *Rochester Times-Chronicle*. He didn't seem too excited about the kittens. "Let's see . . . ah . . . Dora," he said, running his finger down the list of contestants on his clipboard. "You say you're determining the bloodlines of the domestic feline here. Do you have any scientific data?"

"You bet I do," Dora said, pulling out a bunch of photographs. "When Miranda—that's our cat—went into heat, I staked out the barn with my camera and got pictures of all the tomcats that started hanging around."

"Oh, my," Miss Hopewell murmured, her face starting to redden.

Dora picked out a yellow tiger kitten and held it up to one of the snapshots. "This is a picture of Ronald. You can see the strong family resemblance between him and Ronnie Junior. Ronald really gets around. Half the cats in town look just like him."

"Oh, my!" Miss Hopewell said again, a little louder. Mr. Cronmuller clamped his teeth down on the stem of his pipe, and the corners of his mustache twitched.

Dora pulled out two more pictures of possible fathers and matched them up with kittens. "Here's Snowman and Snowflake, and Henrietta is the spitting image of her father, Henry. I offer this as conclusive proof that it is possible for a cat to have a mixed litter as a result of mating with more than one male cat."

"Oh, my gracious," Miss Hopewell exclaimed, giving Miranda a dirty look. Miranda blinked drowsily.

Dora was building up to her grand finale. "And now for my most interesting piece of scientific research. But first I'd like to tell you, Mr. Cronmuller, that I hope to be a photojournalist when I grow up."

"I see," Mr. Cronmuller said through clenched teeth, his smile starting to break through.

Dora held the last picture behind her back. "This photograph will prove, beyond a shadow of a doubt, that even though a male cat may mate with a female cat, it doesn't always result in a kitten that looks like the father. If you will observe the litter, you will see that there are no black kittens. But in this picture," she whipped it out right in front of the judges, "you will see that Inky definitely did—"

"Oh, my good merciful heavens!" Miss Hopewell exclaimed, fanning herself with her clipboard. Mr. Cronmuller laughed right out loud and had to catch his pipe as it fell out of his mouth.

"Here's another picture of Inky, for positive identification," Dora persisted. "You can see his face in this one."

Miss Hopewell shoved Mr. Cronmuller over to our table. "We must be moving on. Thank you, Dora."

Mr. Cronmuller was still laughing. "You might well have a future in photojournalism, young lady," he said over his shoulder. "Your timing is exceptional." He struggled to regain his composure, while Miss Hopewell glared at him.

"The next entry is a working model of a volcano by David Anderson and Sarajane Weiderman," Miss Hopewell said in a shaky voice.

I'd been so busy watching what was going on at the next table, I'd forgotten to uncover the volcano. I fumbled around to find the edge of the plastic wrap and pulled it off. Then Sara dumped the baking soda into the crater, and I followed it right up with the vinegar.

The lava mixture had just started to bubble, when something rose up in the middle of the crater, something that wasn't made out of baking soda and vinegar. It just kept coming up out of the foam.

"Quite an unusual effect," Miss Hopewell said, leaning close for a better look. It wasn't until the flow of lava subsided that we could see what it was. A mouse—with a little mound of baking soda on its head and vinegar dripping off its tiny whiskers. Probably the one that had been living under our sink.

It took a few seconds for Miss Hopewell to recognize it. Then she screamed and sort of folded up like an accordion. Mr. Cronmuller lowered her to the floor and started fanning her face with his clipboard.

The mouse skidded down the slippery slope and jumped off the table. Miranda became instantly alert, and within seconds her nose was just inches from the tip of the mouse's tail. They both scrambled over Miss Hopewell, who looked exactly like our living room sofa now that she was lying down.

Dora ran after Miranda and made a grab for her, knocking over Harold's maze. I saw a little gerbil with the number one on his collar go streaking past my feet. Sara saw it too. "Sludge is fast enough on his own," she said. "Harold didn't need to cheat after all."

Things got pretty confusing after that. Miranda and the mouse managed to wipe out several solar systems and an electromagnetic field before they disappeared out the side door. Sara and I didn't get a blue ribbon after all.

But neither did Dora Simpson.

Chapter 12

"Davey," Mom said. "Have you seen Uncle Will? Your father wants to get home."

Sara and I had been hanging out in the hall since the volcano disaster. We didn't want to run into Miss Hopewell. "I haven't seen him for a while, Mom, but Sara and I can look for him. Do we have time to go get some cookies and stuff in the cafeteria first?"

Dad looked at his watch. He was the only father at the Science Fair with a three-piece suit and a deadline. "Make it snappy, Davey. I have several reports to go over before tomorrow morning. Besides, I think we'd better get you out of here while the school is still standing."

"Don't worry, Dad. The excitement's over. Why don't you come get something to eat? That's probably where Uncle Will is anyway. He loves cookies."

I was right. We found Uncle Will at the refreshment table, having punch and cookies with Mrs. Guptill. He had a big grin on his face, the kind he usually had when he thought he was Willie.

"There you are, Uncle Will," Mom said. "We're

going to be leaving in a few minutes, right after we have some refreshments."

Uncle Will looked disappointed. I thought for sure he was going to start whining like Willie, but he wiped his mouth with a paper napkin and just said, "Well, Jan. I'd sure like it if we could stay a little while longer. I've only polished off about half of these here walnut squares that Mabel brought. I'd hate to miss out on the rest. Mabel is one terrific cook."

I thought I saw Mrs. Guptill blush when he said that. Must have been an optical illusion.

"Maybe he can get a doggie bag," Dad said. "We have to get moving. I'll go pick up Davey's project." Even after all this time, Dad still talked about Uncle Will instead of to him. I don't think he realized he was doing it.

"I can give Will a lift home in the school bus, if you folks want to go on ahead," Mrs. Guptill said, smiling. She looked a lot better when she smiled, not pretty like Mrs. DelVecchio, but definitely better than usual. I watched Uncle Will out of the corner of my eye. I had the feeling he was going to pull a Willie any minute, and I sure didn't want him to be alone with the Water Buffalo when he did it.

I went over to Sara, who was tanking up on punch at the other end of the table. "Hey, Sara," I whispered. "Uncle Will's getting himself into a mess. He's going to ride home on the school bus with Mrs. Guptill."

"What's wrong with that?" she asked, coming up for air with a little lime sherbet mustache.

"You know how Uncle Will is, Sara. What if he starts thinking he's Willie and acts like a jerk in front of her? And there'll be kids on the bus too. What if he does something dumb on the bus and everybody in school hears about it?"

"You worry too much, Davey. First of all, there won't be any kids on the bus. Mrs. Guptill doesn't own a car, so she uses the bus to get around all the time."

"Really? Why is she here, anyway? I thought she was bringing in the kids who didn't have rides to school or something."

Sara shrugged. "No. She always shows up at the school plays and concerts and stuff. I guess she doesn't have much to do at home. She lives by herself."

"There's no Mr. Guptill?"

"No. She's been a widow for as long as I can remember."

Dad came in lugging the volcano. I got back to them just as Mom was saying, "Well, if you're sure it's not too much trouble, Mrs. . . ."

"Guptill," the Water Buffalo said, reaching out her big paw to shake hands with Mom. "Just call me Mabel. And no, it's no trouble at all. It would be a pleasure. Will and me are becoming real good friends. Aren't we, Will?"

Uncle Will had just stuffed a whole walnut square into his mouth, so all he could do was bob his head up and down and smile. He looked like an overgrown chipmunk.

I couldn't think of any way to keep Uncle Will from going home with Mrs. Guptill, but he seemed okay at the moment, so I figured it didn't matter. I looked back over my shoulder as we left the room.

Uncle Will was helping himself to another walnut square, and he was whispering something into Mrs. Guptill's ear. I could swear she was blushing again.

When we got home, I took the volcano up to my room, but Brad stopped me at the door. "You're not bringing that stupid thing in here."

"Why not? It's my room, too."

"Yeah, I know. But I need a lot of space right now to work on my airplane model. Dad's taking me to a meet next weekend, so I have to get it finished." Brad's model airplane stuff was spread out all over the long table we were supposed to share as a desk.

"Half of that table is mine," I said, pushing past him. "How am I supposed to do my homework if you're taking up the whole desk?"

Brad grabbed my arm. "Don't give me that. The only place you ever do homework is downstairs in front of the TV. If you touch any of this stuff, I'll break your arm." He let go of me and gently lifted the balsa wood frame of an airplane. "This one's going to be a real prize winner."

"I still say half of the desk is mine, Brad. Move your junk over."

"No way, pipsqueak. Sharing a room with you wasn't my idea. Besides, you shouldn't get half of the desk anyway. I'm older, so I get more space."

"Being older doesn't have anything to do with how much space you get, except maybe floor space for your big feet." That was a sore point with Brad. He had the biggest shoe size of anybody in the high school. He could practically water-ski in his bare feet.

"All right, that does it. I'll figure this out

mathematically." Brad shuffled through his junk and came up with a pad and pencil and a ruler. "You're eleven and I'm fifteen and the desk is . . ." He measured the desk with his ruler and wrote something on the pad. ". . . forty-eight and five-eighths inches wide . . . so that means, if you're only eleven-fifteenths as old as I am, your share of the desk would be . . . seven times three is twenty-one, carry the two . . . plus five to the third power . . . divided by four and three-eighths . . ."

He was running around like a maniac, measuring and figuring, and then he started marking boundaries with chalk. Not just the desk, but the whole room.

"Okay, your share of the desk is seventeen and nine-sixteenth inches," he said with a sly smile. He made a big deal about moving one of his airplanes over the chalk line to his side.

"That's not fair. That doesn't give me room to do anything."

"How much room do you need for follow-the-dots and color-in-the-three-red-apples? Wait until you have real homework, like Biology and Afro-Asian. Then see how much room you need. Besides, according to this, I own the bottom nine inches of your bed, which I'm willing to turn over to you. And I'm also giving you a right of way from the door through my property to your side of the room. So don't say I'm not being fair about this."

"That's stupid," I shouted. "How could you own part of my bed?"

He held up the pad with all the numbers on it and slapped it with the back of his hand. "It's all here in black and white. You want to do the calculations yourself?"

"I'm going to tell Mom. Share means half."

"Oh, yeah? Well, while you're at it, why don't you tell Mom to dump that crazy old uncle of hers in a nursing home, so we can live a normal life around here for a change?"

"We don't have a chance for a normal life around here with you living in the house," I yelled. "Uncle Will isn't crazy and he isn't the problem. It's you. You're . . . you're . . . abnormal!"

I heard Brad snort as I grabbed my homework and ran down the stairs. I never could think of a good exit line when I fought with him.

Dad was sitting at the desk in the living room working on his reports. Mom was on the couch, waiting for the Wednesday-night movie to start, so I settled in next to her. Pretty soon, Brad came downstairs and plunked himself in Uncle Will's chair.

"The temperature's really dropping tonight," Dad said. "I heard the furnace kick on a few minutes ago."

"I don't feel any heat yet," Mom said.

"The heat run for this room is over by Uncle Will's chair," Dad explained. "It'll take a while to warm up the room."

"Speaking of Uncle Will," Mom said, "he's been gone quite a while. I wonder when that Mrs. Guptill will bring him back."

Brad grinned. "Guptill? Uncle Will is out with the Water Buffalo again?" Brad snickered as he slouched his long body down into the chair. Then he started squirming around and jumped up. "Geez! This chair still stinks. Didn't you wash the cat pee off this thing, Mom?"

Mom went over to the chair and took a sniff. "I thought we'd solved the problem. Your father and I scrubbed it down with everything we could think of. You're right, though. There is a definite odor."

"Uncle Will must have kept at least half a dozen cats in that house, from what I could see," Dad said. "The chair probably has been saturated over the years. All our scrubbing just took care of the outside. Sitting right next to the heat run like that is going to make the odor even more noticeable."

Mom studied the chair. "Maybe if I made a slipcover for it . . ."

"Yeah, Mom," Brad said, heading for the kitchen and the refrigerator. "Maybe you could whip something up out of Odor Eaters."

Dad looked up from his papers. "A slipcover wouldn't do anything, Jan. You'd just be wasting your time. The only answer is to get rid of the old thing."

Mom straightened up and glared at Dad. "You're referring to the chair, I presume?"

Dad stared back at her for a few seconds before answering. Then he spoke very slowly. "That's one solution, yes. I'm sure we could both think of an alternate plan that would work out better for everyone concerned." Mom's eyebrow shot up so far I thought it would get stuck there.

Just then we heard the back door open. Uncle Will was home. He came into the living room and brought Mrs. Guptill with him. Mom got a guilty look on her face and started running off at the mouth. "Oh, Uncle Will . . . and Mrs. Guptill. Did you have a nice time?"

Uncle Will grinned. "Sure did. Mabel took me for a spin around town in that bus of hers. She's got the inside fixed up real purty."

Mom beamed. "That's nice, Uncle Will. Isn't that nice, John?"

Dad mumbled something into his papers.

Mom was flitting around playing Mrs. Hostess. "Please come in and sit down. Could I get you some coffee?"

Mrs. Guptill took a couple of steps backward. "Thanks just the same, Mrs. Anderson, but I've got to get home. Have to be up bright and early for the first morning run."

Uncle Will took her hand. "Thanks for bringing me home, Mabel. And thanks for them walnut squares. I've got the last few stashed in my pocket," he said, patting his back pants pocket. I hoped he remembered to take them out before he sat down. The way he was gazing into Mrs. Guptill's eyes, you would have thought he was in love with her or something. She must be one fantastic cook. He walked her out to the bus, then came back into the living room.

Mom jumped up again. "We were just talking about you before you came in, Uncle Will. We were thinking that your birthday is coming up soon and we'd like to get you something special. Something you'd really use."

"Ain't nothin' I need," he said, easing himself down into his chair. He sort of dropped the last few inches, making the cushion release a new puff of cat odor and a rude noise. So much for those walnut squares.

"Well, that's just it," Mom continued, her hands starting to flutter. "We'd like to replace something you already have . . . this chair."

Uncle Will rubbed both hands along the arms of the chair where it was already worn smooth and shiny from years of use. "This chair's an old friend," he said quietly. "It'll last as long as I'll be needing a place to sit."

"But there are much nicer ones now," Mom persisted. "There are lounge chairs with footrests that come up. Some of them operate by a push button."

"Naw. I ain't much for fancy things, Jan."

Mom didn't seem to hear him. She was on a roll. "They have chairs with buttons to operate the TV, and they even have a kind with a motor in it to give you a massage."

"If I take a notion to have a massage, I don't want to get it from no chair," Uncle Will said, frowning.

"Maybe we could just go to a furniture store so you could see what I'm talking about. You might find one that you really—"

Uncle Will heaved himself up out of the chair. The cushion inhaled. "I don't want some dang newfangled chair with buttons. Only place I want buttons is on my shirt."

"Oh, Uncle Will, I'm sorry. I just thought—"

Uncle Will was getting red in the face, waving his arms around. "That old chair don't do nothin' fancy. It just sits. That's what chairs and useless old men are supposed to do. Just sit!" With that, he turned and stormed out of the room.

Chapter 13

When I arrived home from school the next day, Mom was in the backyard raking leaves. She stopped and wiped her forehead. "You know, Davey, all this country space is terrific, but it's a lot more work than I ever imagined. How about grabbing the other rake and giving me a hand?"

"Okay, Mom," I said. "Just let me dump my stuff in the house first."

"I left a snack for you on the kitchen table—artichoke chips."

"Artichoke chips?"

"Yes, they look almost like potato chips, but they're made out of Jerusalem artichokes. I found a whole patch of them growing behind the barn. I looked them up in my *Growing Unique Vegetables* book, and it says they're a marvelous low-calorie substitute for potatoes. Don't eat too many, though. The book says they can give you gas."

"Okay, Mom. I'll try to restrain myself," I said, heading for the kitchen door. I had the feeling Uncle Will and I might be going out to murder some artichokes soon.

Before I even reached the door, I knew something was wrong. I could hear the beep of the smoke alarm in the kitchen. I felt the door to make sure it wasn't hot, then yanked it open. There was a thick layer of smoke about three feet thick, hanging up by the ceiling. It was coming from the stove.

Mom must have heard the smoke alarm when I opened the door, because she was right behind me. She pushed me out of the way and ran for the stove. "It's this pan," she yelled. She turned off the burner and grabbed the pan off the stove with a potholder, running back to fling it out into the driveway. "Open up those windows, Davey. I'll get Uncle Will. He must be in his room."

Just then we heard coughing, and Uncle Will stumbled into the kitchen, looking bewildered.

Mom took him by the arm and led him toward the door. "Come on, Uncle Will. Let's get out of this smoke."

Uncle Will moved like a sleepwalker with his arms groping in front of him. He didn't seem to know where he was. "What? What's going on?"

"We have to get outside, Uncle Will. Just come with me out into the fresh air. It's too smoky to stay in here." Mom was real gentle with Uncle Will, coaxing him along until we were all outside. Then she let him have it. "You put water on for coffee and forgot it again, didn't you, Uncle Will?"

Uncle Will rubbed his forehead. "I . . . I don't know. I don't think so. I was just taking a nap."

"Look," Mom said, her eyes flashing. "You and I were the only two people at home, and I know I didn't put any water on, so that just leaves you. Besides, that's the third or fourth time you've put water on the stove and forgotten it. Up until now, I've just found it boiling like mad, but today. . ." She picked up the charred pan and shook it in his face. "Today you could have burned the house down."

Uncle Will held up his hands. "I'm sorry, Jan. I didn't mean—"

"I know you didn't mean any harm, but the point is, this could have been a disaster. I've asked you over and over again to use the microwave when you want coffee."

I felt really sorry for Uncle Will. I knew he hadn't burned the pot on purpose. He just forgot things sometimes.

As if the whole scene weren't bad enough, Dad's car pulled into the driveway. "What's happening? I smell something burning," Dad yelled as he jumped out of the car.

I tried to head him off. "Don't worry, Dad. It was just a little accident, but everything's okay."

"Everything is *not* okay," Mom said. "Uncle Will just came within minutes of burning the house down."

"Aw, Mom, he just burned a pot."

"Did he forget his coffee water again?" Dad asked, his jaw set in a grim line.

"I've asked him over and over to use the microwave, but no, he has to use the stove."

Uncle Will scowled. "I can't use that contraption. It ain't natural. I don't use any piece of machinery unless I know how it works."

Mom practically screamed at Uncle Will. "Nobody understands how a microwave works. For all I know, there could be little elves in there. It doesn't matter how it works! Just fill a mug with water and put it in the microwave on 'high' for two minutes. Is that so hard to remember?"

Uncle Will didn't say anything.

"Well, is it?" Mom yelled.

"Goldang it!" Uncle Will yelled. "Everything's gettin' hard to remember." He turned and headed back into the house, slamming the screen door behind him.

Mom clenched her fists and started to cry. "Why does he have to be so blasted stubborn? He never used to be like this."

Dad put his arms around her. "He's getting old, Jan. People change. His mind is going, and he'll probably get worse instead of better."

It was hard to imagine how things could get much worse. I slipped back into the house and opened up a few more windows. The smell of smoke still hung in all the rooms. I opened up the front door and tried swinging it back and forth like a big fan for a few minutes to move the air around. Then I went upstairs to check on Uncle Will.

His door wasn't closed all the way, but I knocked anyway.

"Come on in."

I poked my head around the door. He was sitting on his bed looking at an old scrapbook.

"Hi, Uncle Will. I just wanted to make sure you were all right."

"Sure, I'm fine." He patted the bed. "Come here a minute, Davey. I want to show you something."

I sat next to him, and he moved half of the scrapbook onto my lap.

He pointed to a picture, tapping it several times with his gnarled finger. "You know who that is?"

It was a black-and-white photo of a little girl and a man about Dad's age. The girl was wearing one of those costumes that ballerinas wear, with a sparkly crown on her head. The man was in a white suit, with white shoes that had a black design on the toes. He held her hand, bowing, and she was doing a curtsy, looking up at him. An older woman and another man were sitting in the background, laughing and clapping. There was something familiar about the face of the man in the white suit. "Is that you?" I asked.

"You bet it is. That's me in my ice-cream suit. That's what we used to call them fancy white suits."

"Who's the little girl?"

"That's my little Janny girl."

"Mom?"

"Yep."

"No kidding. Why is she in that costume? Was it Halloween?"

"Nope. We were doing our annual Stark Follies." He laughed. "Yessir, every summer your mother and your grandparents would come to pay us a visit for two weeks. Jan would bring her costume from her ballet recital, and she'd start in on me as soon as she got out of the car. 'We have to start rehearsing, Uncle Will,' she'd say, and she'd drag me into the big old parlor, the one with no rug on the floor. She called it the ballroom." He chuckled softly to himself. "The ballroom . . . that's what she called it." He sort of drifted off into his thoughts for a few minutes.

"So you and Mom put on some kind of a show? I didn't even know she could dance."

He brightened up again. "She sure could, and she could make up her own dances, too. We'd go through all the records and pick out the ones we wanted to use. We had one of them old wind-up victrolas. Then every day, as soon as I got cleaned up from my morning chores, Janny and I would start rehearsing."

"You danced too?"

"Yep. Not the ballet stuff like your mother, but I could waltz better than any man in the county."

"Can you still? Waltz?"

"I don't know. Haven't had much call for waltzing lately." His eyes looked sad again.

"Who came to see your show, Uncle Will?"

"Just the family—Ma, my brother Ray, and your grandparents. We always had it on the last night before they had to go back home. And we made everybody dress up too, like they was going to a regular concert. Even Ray, and he wasn't much for fancyin' up. To hear him, you'd think a necktie was a noose."

"I bet you had fun," I said, shifting my position. My feet were starting to fall asleep.

"Yep," he said. "Those were good times . . . real good times." He took off his glasses and rubbed his hand back and forth over his eyes. Then I saw his lower lip start to tremble.

"You okay, Uncle Will?"

"They're all gone now, Davey. Even the farm. The only ones left is me and Jan. But she's not the same anymore." He shook his head. "She's not the Janny who used to look up to me."

I didn't know what to say. "People change," I mumbled.

All of a sudden Uncle Will started to cry. Not just tears, but big sobs that shook his whole body. "Why should she look up to me? Look what I've turned into. I've . . . I've gone and lost everything . . . let everybody down. Let it all slip away."

"No you haven't, Uncle Will." I reached around behind him and patted his back, like Mom always did to me when I was upset.

"I'm a stupid good-for-nothing old fool. I couldn't save Ma . . . couldn't save Ray, and I . . . I couldn't even save our farm. I never took help from nobody before, but now I'm a beat-up old failure."

"It wasn't your fault, Uncle Will," I said, crying myself now. "It just happened, that's all. You're a good person." I hugged him hard. "I love you," I whispered, and we cried together while the shadows stretched long across the floor of his room.

Chapter 14

Sara never even looked at me coming home on the school bus the next day, but as soon as the bus pulled away, she said, "Come into the barn, Davey. I have a surprise for you."

"What kind of a surprise?" I asked, hoping for double fudge chocolate-chip brownies.

"Oh, nothing important," she said, skipping backward in front to me. "Just the total, complete and perfect answer to getting back at those rotten Spiders, that's all." She smiled mysteriously.

"What do you have? A nuclear weapon?" I asked, following her through the barn door.

"This," she said, reaching for something in the shadowy corner of an empty stall. She held it up.

"A book?" I said. "How's that going to solve our problems with the Spiders? They probably can't even read." Sara just smiled and held the book up in front of me. I looked closer. The title was *How Karate Can Change Your Life*.

"Oh, no, Sara. I'm not going to take on those guys with karate. They'd kill me. Besides, I look like a wimp in pajamas."

Sara wasn't paying any attention to me. She licked the tip of her index finger and began turning the pages. "We'll start with something simple, like breaking a cement block in half with your bare hand."

"No way!" I yelled.

"Oh, all right," she said. "A board, then."

"Forget it!"

"Well, if you're not willing to start with the simple stuff, we'll have to get right into the more advanced moves. Let's try this one where you flip your opponent over."

Sara set the book down on a bale of hay and started imitating the position of the guy in the picture. "Okay, Davey. Just stand still while I try to figure this out."

"Oh, sure, Sara. That's how I'll start out with the Spiders. I'll say, 'Hey, Lester, just stand still while I figure out how to flip you on your stupid head, okay? And Leo, would you be so kind as to hold this book up so I can see it? Yeah, Leo. This is called a book. *B-o-o-k*. See the pretty pictures?'"

"You'll thank me for this, Davey," Sara said, coming toward me. She was in a half-squatting position with her legs apart like a frog's, and she kept jumping from side to side looking at me first over one shoulder, then the other.

"Sara, the only way this would work on the Spiders is if they laughed themselves to death. You look like a total—" Suddenly Sara yelled something, and the whole barn tipped over—just tipped over on its side, so I was looking straight at the hayloft and rafters. It took a second or two for me to realize that I was the one who had done the tipping. I was lying flat on my back.

Sara stood above me with her hands on her hips. "Ha!" she said. "Works like a charm. I told you it would."

"How did you do that?" I asked, sitting up and checking for broken bones. "I didn't even feel you touch me."

Sara grinned. "I know. Isn't it amazing? Here. I'll show you how. Follow me." She squat-hopped across the barn floor and I followed, trying my best to imitate her. I felt like a frog.

"Now you do it alone," she said.

"Come on, Sara. This is stupid."

"Do you or do you not want to make mincemeat out of the Spiders?"

"Well, sure, but I don't see how jumping around like an idiot is going to do it."

"Trust me," she said. "And this time, add a yell at the end."

She squinted at me critically as I made a solo trip across the barn. When I was right in front of her, I yelled, "Watch out!"

Sara hit her forehead with the palm of her hand. "Watch out? You don't yell 'watch out,' for pete's sake!"

"Well, what am I supposed to yell?"

"Something Japanese."

"Why didn't you say so in the first place?" I went back to the starting position. This time, just as I got to Sara, I yelled, "Toyota!"

Sara let out a disgusted sigh. "Honestly, Davey. I

thought you were a lot smarter than most other boys."

"Well, excuse me, Sara, but my Japanese vocabulary is a bit limited. *Toyota* and *Kawasaki* are about it, okay?"

"It doesn't have to be real Japanese. Just say something that sounds Japanese. You don't want them to know what you're saying, anyway. That's part of the element of surprise. Say something like 'ee-jah-wah.'"

"That's dumb," I countered.

Sara ignored my remark. "This time, just after you yell, duck down like this and grab me right here. As you push on past me, I'll flip right over your shoulder."

I went back into my starting position.

"That's pretty good, Davey, but you don't look mean enough," Sara said.

I raised one side of my upper lip in a half snarl.

"Great!" Sara exclaimed.

I know I did everything right—the snarl, the squat-hop, and the yell—but something happened with the flip part. Sara didn't flip. She just collapsed on top of me. Four different times!

"That does it," I said finally. "If I can't flip somebody your size, I don't stand a chance of budging the Spiders at all."

Sara slumped down on a bale of hay. "I'm afraid you may be right, Davey. You don't show much of an aptitude for karate. You're getting really good at the yelling, though. That's probably the most important part anyway." Sara jumped up and started pacing, something I noticed she often did when she was coming up with a plan.

Suddenly her face lit up. "I've got it," she shouted. "We'll forget the karate, except maybe for the yell, which is quite effective, and we'll try swashbuckling."

"What the heck is swashbuckling?"

"I saw it in an old movie on TV. This guy—a pirate—wiped out a whole bunch of bad guys by swinging on a rope and busting them in the gut with his feet."

"I thought the pirates *were* the bad guys," I said.

"Don't change the subject, Davey. This is perfect. How much do you weigh?"

"I don't know. Around eighty pounds, I guess."

"Terrific. Don't you see? You use your weight instead of your muscles. You just yell 'ee-jah-wah,' then swing through the air and get them in the stomach with an eighty-pound blow. They'll never know what hit them. Come on. Let's practice."

There was a rope hanging from the main rafter that we sometimes used for swinging into the soft pile of hay at the other end of the barn. We climbed up to the loft and Sara swung first, yelling "ee-jah-wah" at the top of her lungs. She dropped into the hay below, then dragged a fresh bale of hay into the center of the pile. "Pretend this is Lester, Davey. Let's see you nail him."

On the first swing I sailed right past "Lester" and landed in the hay.

"Aim next time, will you?" Sara said, standing a

second bale of hay next to the first. "There. If you aim for Lester, you might at least get Leo by mistake."

"Very funny," I said. "It's not that easy to steer a rope, you know."

"It's not that easy to rope a steer either," Sara said. "You just have to practice until you get the hang of it."

After a few more tries, I got Lester, and the time after that I got Leo. Pretty soon I could get Leo on the swing over and Lester on the swing back. Then I started doing two-in-ones, picking them both off in one swing.

After about a half hour, all the yelling and swashbuckling sort of went to my head. I began to think of myself as invincible. That's why, when Sara suggested we set a trap for the Spiders in the woods, I went along with it. I even thought it sounded like a great idea. That's what swashbuckling can do to a guy.

We went back in the woods, to the place where the Spiders had ambushed us, and found the rope they had used to tie us up.

"There's a perfect tree, Davey." Sara was pointing to a huge old maple. "It's just around the bend in the path, so the Spiders can't see you hiding in it until they get really close." We climbed the tree and tied a big, heavy rope to one of the branches. Luckily, I had learned about knots a couple of years back in Cub Scouts. I tied the rope to the limb with a timber hitch. Then I made a big stevedore knot and added a stopper knot right below it for a "seat." When it was ready, I tried it out. I made a perfect swashbuckle, arching across the path with my feet at Spider-stomach height. Nothing could stop me now. Confident, we ran back to Sara's house to lure the Spiders.

Sara looked up the Spiders' number and dialed it. "It's ringing," she whispered. "Could I speak with Lester, please? . . . A friend from school."

Sara covered the mouthpiece. "That was his mother. She's calling him. . . . Oh, my gosh. She's calling him 'sweetie pie.' Do you believe it? Sweetie pie? Lester?" Sara closed her eyes and tried not to laugh. I had to turn my face toward the wall and put both hands over my mouth. I snorted.

"Shh," Sara said, laughing. "I can hear him coming. Here he is!" She made her voice low and mysterious. "Hello, Lester . . . Wouldn't you like to know? . . . Just a friend . . . Knock it off, you creep!"

She put her hand over the mouthpiece. "You wouldn't believe what that jerk just said to me. I'm going to drop the sexy voice." She took her hand away from the receiver and spoke in her normal voice, which definitely was not sexy.

"Listen, Lester. It's time for you and your dumb brother to show how brave you are. You are being challenged to a fight. . . . By Davey Anderson, that's who. . . . Of course I don't sound like Davey Anderson."

She covered the receiver again and rolled her eyes. "Lester is so dumb." Then back into the phone: "This is his personal secretary speaking. I personally make all his appointments. . . . No, he can't come to the phone . . . because he is mentally preparing for battle, that's why. . . . Davey Anderson is skilled in the ancient ritual of ee-jah-wah."

We both started laughing. Sara had to bite her lip. "I didn't expect a dumb person like you to know what that is. . . . You'll have to meet at the appointed place if you want to find out . . . in Anderson's woods. . . . You'll know the spot when you get there. . . . Davey Anderson will be waiting."

She hung up, then jumped up and down, laughing. "He bought it. They're coming. Come on. You have to get up in the tree before they get there."

We ran into the woods, still laughing. Sara hid in a clump of bushes, and I took my place on the branch below the one where the rope was tied. I yanked on it a few times to make sure the knot was secure. It was. Then Sara and I waited, motionless, listening for the Spiders.

After what seemed like an hour, I said, "Maybe they chickened out."

"They'll come," Sara said. "The Spiders wouldn't miss the chance for a good fight."

I looked down at the ground. It looked a lot farther than it had before. "What time is it?" I asked.

"Four-thirty," Sara answered. "And be quiet. They'll be here any minute."

Four-thirty. That meant it had been about a half hour since my last swashbuckle. The spell seemed to be wearing off. My hands were getting sweaty. I wiped them on my jacket. I could feel my heart starting to beat faster.

Just then I heard them. They were arguing as they crunched through the dry leaves on the path. Sounds carry for a long distance in the woods, so I kept expecting them to pop around the bend any second, but the path stayed empty. Then, without warning, they were right under me, as if somebody had waved a magic wand and *poof!* Spiders!

I took a deep breath and yelled as I grabbed the rope and started the longest swashbuckle of my life. I heard the word *Toyotahhhhh* stretch out behind me as I swung through the air. Sara would get me later for that. I never could remember my lines under pressure.

I kept my eyes riveted on Lester's stomach as I headed for him. He was wearing a T-shirt that said I LIVE FOR ROCK AND ROLL. I could tell it was going to be a direct hit. It was. When my sneakers connected with Lester's shirt, right on the word ROLL, he folded in half with a loud whoosh of air. I looked over my shoulder to locate Leo so I could get him on my second swing. It was then I realized there wasn't going to be a second swing.

The bales of hay had just toppled over when I hit them, so I could keep swinging and pick off another bale. The human body didn't do that. Crashing into Lester had stopped all of my momentum. I was just hanging there in mid-air, and Leo was closing in on me.

I frantically swung my legs back and forth, but I couldn't start swinging again. I just twisted in the wind, like a lynching victim.

Even Lester was coming around now, getting to his feet with pure hate in his eyes. I considered dropping to the ground and running, but the Spiders were coming at me from both directions on the path, and the underbrush was too thick to get through on either side. I made one frantic last-ditch effort at leg swinging, and then it happened. Just as Leo reached me, I managed to swing past him, and at the same instant, there was a loud cracking sound. The limb holding the rope gave way, and both Spiders disappeared in a blur of branches and orange leaves.

"Sara!" I yelled. "Let's make a run for it."

The Spiders were already struggling out from under the branches as Sara and I headed for the bridge. We never looked back until we were safely inside our house. Dad was in the kitchen, so Sara and I went into the living room, where we could talk in private. Before long, there was a knock at the back door. Dad answered it.

We heard a gruff voice say, "You got a kid named Davey?" Sara and I crept over to peek into the kitchen and saw a square, muscular man with black hair.

"Why, yes," Dad said. "What seems to be the problem?"

"Look what your kid and his friends did to my kids. Ganged up on 'em and beat 'em up. Look at 'em. All scraped up. Leo here had a bloody nose. I oughta sue."

"I don't understand," Dad said. "Davey did that to these boys?"

"Yeah. He did that," the man said. "Just now. Him and his gang. Bring him out here. I seen your kid before. He must be almost six feet tall. Why's a big kid like that picking on younger kids? I oughta wallop him myself."

"I wouldn't do that, if I were you," Dad said. "Davey, come out here, will you?"

I went into the kitchen. Mr. Snyder's jaw dropped. "What? Hey, wait a minute. This ain't Davey. This here's just a little kid. I want to talk to the big guy."

"You must have seen our older son, Brad. I'm

afraid he couldn't have been involved in the fight. He's playing in a basketball game in Williamson this afternoon." Dad turned to me. I could tell he was trying not to smile. "Davey? Mr. Snyder says you beat up his sons. Is that right?"

There didn't seem to be much sense in lying, so I didn't. "Yeah, Dad," I said.

Mr. Snyder looked at the Spiders. "This is who beat you up? You come home crying like babies over being beat up by a . . . a pipsqueak like this?"

I looked closer at the Spiders. Tearstains streaked their dirty faces. "He didn't do it alone, Dad," Lester whined. "He had a bunch of friends with him. Big guys. They jumped us."

"Is that true, Davey?" Dad asked.

"There was only one other person, Dad."

"Who?"

"Me," Sara said, stepping into the kitchen.

Mr. Snyder's face turned dark red. "A girl? You mealy-mouthed little cowards got beat up by a midget and a . . . *girl?*" He grabbed each one of them by the ear and marched them out the door, still yelling. "You two can just forget about the Marines. They're not going to let any lily-livered sissies join up. No sir. You can just forget about the family tradition. Three generations of Snyders in the Marines, but not you two. . . ." His voice faded off in the distance, and the Spiders walked, or rather were dragged, out of our lives for good.

Chapter 15

A few mornings later, I went back upstairs after breakfast and stretched out on my bed. This was my favorite time of day, after Brad left on the early bus. I was just enjoying having the room to myself when there was a knock on the door.

"Come in."

Uncle Will came in carrying two coffee mugs. He handed one to me and sat down at the table. "Thought you might like to have your morning coffee in bed," he said. "Made it myself in that Michaelwave contraption." He grinned and sipped from his mug.

I'd never had a cup of coffee in my life, but I didn't want to hurt his feelings. I'd been so busy with Sara and the Spiders, I hadn't even had time to think about Uncle Will since the pot-burning incident. I felt guilty about that, because I'd planned to try to make him feel more at home.

"Gee, thanks, Uncle Will. It smells great. How's everything going with you?"

"Oh, pretty well," he said, poking around at Brad's airplane stuff. I almost asked him to leave it alone. Then I remembered how broken up he'd been after Mom yelled at him, and I let it go. I took a sip of the coffee. It was so bitter, it made me shiver.

Uncle Will picked up the balsa wood airplane frame and turned it around and around in his hands. "I used to build these things when I was a boy," he said. "You make this one?"

"No, that's Brad's. He won't let me touch his stuff. He gets real mad if *anybody* messes with his planes."

I hoped Uncle Will would take the hint. He didn't. Just then Mom called up the stairs. "Davey! You'd better hurry or you'll miss the bus."

"Guess I won't be able to finish the coffee," I said, grabbing my books. "I'll have to run. Mrs. Guptill is always on time."

Uncle Will's face brightened. "Maybe I'll tag along after you and wave to Mabel as she goes by."

I ran on ahead and was already at the bus stop by the time Mrs. Guptill passed our house. I could see Uncle Will at the end of the driveway, waving. The Water Buffalo waved back, and she still had a big smile on her face as she reached the stop.

When I got home that afternoon, the house was empty. I figured Mom must have taken Uncle Will along while she did her errands. I went to the refrigerator and gulped some milk out of the carton, something I wouldn't do if Mom was around, and headed up to my room. I was in a pretty good mood, now that we didn't have to worry about the Spiders bugging me anymore. Sara and I could ruin their reputations at school if we told about the scene with their father, and the Spiders knew it. We had them right where we wanted them. I was whistling to myself as I climbed the stairs, but my good mood changed when I opened the door to my room.

Uncle Will was sitting at the table, hunched over Brad's plane, trying to stretch a piece of bright red tissue over the frame. He was concentrating so hard he didn't see me at first, and his tongue worked its way around his mouth as he pulled at the sticky paper. The wing of the plane was already covered with tissue, but it was all wrinkled and twisted, not stretched tight and smooth the way it was when Brad did it.

"What the heck are you doing?" I yelled.

Uncle Will jumped and pulled his hands away from the plane, but his fingers were so coated with glue, a part of the tissue ripped away and stuck to his hand. "Don't yell at me, Ray. You scare me when you yell like that. I was just helping you fix up your airplane. See?" He picked up the ruined plane and held it out to me, smiling. "Isn't it pretty? I made it red, Ray. Your favorite color."

"I told you Brad didn't want anybody messing with his plane," I shouted. "Now you've wrecked it. He's worked on this thing for weeks, and you've put the tissue on all wrinkled and messed up."

"I can fix that, Ray. Watch me." Uncle Will patted at the tissue on one wing, and it became stuck to his fingers. Then, before I could stop him, he tried to shake it off his hand, and the wing tip twisted and splintered. "I can fix it. I can fix it. I can fix it," he chanted frantically. He picked up the broken wing piece and tried to jam it back on to the fuselage, cracking more of the thin balsa wood struts.

I grabbed what was left of the plane away from him and put it down on the table. "Just leave it alone," I shouted. "You're only making it worse."

Uncle Will pulled at the piece of red tissue that was stuck to his right hand. He got it off, but then it was stuck to his left hand. He kept tugging back and forth at it until little pieces were attached to all of his fingers. He started crying. "I didn't mean to hurt nuthin'. I just wanted to help. I just wanted to do somethin' nice for somebody. For you, Ray. I wanted to do somethin' nice for you."

"Look, Uncle Will, or Willie or whoever you are. I'm not Ray. I'm Davey. Got that? And you're not a little kid. You're an old man." I grabbed his arm and pulled him over in front of the mirror on Brad's dresser. "See that? There's only one kid in that mirror, and that's me, Davey. The other one is you. You're Will Stark and you're seventy-four years old."

Uncle Will covered his face with his hands. "Don't be mean, Ray," he whined.

I grabbed one of his hands away from his face and held my hand next to it. "Look, Uncle Will. Look at our hands. Yours is wrinkled and spotted. That's not the hand of a kid."

He turned his head away. "You're playin' tricks on me, Ray. I'm goin' to tell Ma."

"Come on, Uncle Will," I yelled. "You've got to shape up. If you keep messing up like this, Mom and Dad are going to send you to a nursing home."

"No!" Uncle Will wailed. "Nobody's sending me to no home. I've got my own home. I'm goin' there right now. This is a bad place. I'm gettin' out of here."

Before I could say anything, he pushed past me and ran down the stairs. He stormed out the back door and headed for the woods. I stayed with him this time. I figured I could get him calmed down after a while and get him back home. Just beyond the bridge, I caught up with him and grabbed his arm.

"I didn't mean to yell at you, Uncle Will. Come on back home with me, okay?"

His eyes were red-rimmed from crying and kind of glazed over. "I'm goin' home. Ain't nobody can stop me. I'm goin' home." He shook his arm away from my grip and stumbled down the path.

I stayed close behind him, but I couldn't get him to stop. "Please come back with me, Willie. You're going to get lost."

He kept mumbling, "I'm goin' home," over and over.

Before we got to Sara's house, he turned off the path and started heading south, through the thick brush. We were going away from Berg Road now, into an area where there was nothing but woods for miles. I started to panic because I couldn't recognize any landmarks.

"Come on, Willie. Let's go back," I said. "I'll take you to the soda fountain."

"Goin' home," he whispered in a hoarse, raspy voice. "Goin' home."

"A vanilla phosphate, Willie."

"Goin' home. Goin' home."

I don't know how long we kept pushing on through the woods. I stopped a few times to make trail markers, little piles of rocks and broken branches pointing the way, but I had lost my bearings. There wasn't any way to tell which direction was home, because the sky had clouded over, and there weren't any shadows to judge the position of the sun.

I had lost sight of Uncle Will when I stopped to make my last trail marker, but I could hear him thrashing through the underbrush. "Willie!" I called. "Wait up!" There was no answer, and the thrashing continued. I called a few more times, but he either didn't hear me or wouldn't listen. I knew I had to go for help now, because we'd both be lost if I kept trying to track him. I turned around and started following my trail markers back home.

I was going pretty well for a while, watching for my markers and the trail in between where we had trampled the underbrush. Then I came to the section where I hadn't started to mark the trail, and I knew I was lost.

I kept going, walking in what I thought was a straight line, but after a while I came back to the same twisted little tree I'd seen about a half hour before. I sat down and listened. There was no sound from Uncle Will anymore. I heard a flock of geese flying overhead, but I couldn't even use the geese as a sign and figure they were flying south. The geese in our area had just flown over Lake Ontario from Canada, and half the time they were flying east or west. Uncle Will had told me it was because they were hungry and looking for feeding spots.

Even though I really wanted to get up and start moving, I made myself stay still a while longer. That's what they had told us to do in Scouts. I listened real hard, and pretty soon I could barely make out the sound of running water. The creek! If I could follow it, I could get back to our bridge. I headed in the direction of the sound, stopping every few feet to make sure it was getting closer.

Finally I pushed through a thick section of brush, and there it was, the water rushing over big rocks. I wasn't behind our house, though. There was just a big, empty field and the road beyond it. I found a fallen log lying across the creek and used it as a bridge. When I got out to the road, I saw where I was, almost up to the main highway, at least a couple of miles from home. I started walking, pulling up my collar to shield my ears from the brisk wind that had come up. The clouds were clearing out now, but the sun was too far down to warm anything. It just gave the sky in the west a rosy glow as it disappeared behind the woods.

I remembered that Uncle Will had gone out without a jacket, just a thin flannel shirt. Now that it was getting dark, we might not find him in time. He could freeze to death. As tired as I was, I started running.

The last streaks of pink were fading in the sky, and I was still a long way from home when I saw the familiar shape of a school bus coming toward me. The only bus driver that would be out this time of night had to be Mrs. Guptill. She could at least get me home so we could call for help. I stood in the road and started waving my arms to stop her. For once I was glad my jacket was neon orange. I saw her yellow lights flash, then the red ones as she pulled to a stop and opened the door.

"Davey?" she yelled. "What in tarnation are you doing out in the middle of the road?"

I was so out of breath I could hardly talk. "Uncle Will," I gasped as I scrambled up the steps into the bus.

"Will? Will Stark? What about him?"

"He's lost in the woods. He just kept going, and I couldn't stop him, and then I got lost and . . ."

I almost fell over as Mrs. Guptill hung a U-turn in the middle of Lakeside Road. Not many people could do that with a school bus. She gunned the engine and picked up the mike to her CB radio. "Breaker, breaker on channel ten. This is Able Mabel. Anybody copy?"

A crackly voice came over the radio. "Red Rooster back to you, Able Mabel. What're you up to tonight? Over."

"You're just the person I hoped to scare up, Red Rooster. We got ourselves a problem here. There's a man lost in the woods somewhere between Lakeside and County Line. Can you hop up to channels eleven and twelve and see how many of the other school bus drivers you can rouse? We're going to need a big search party to cover that area. Over."

"Ten-four, Able Mabel. Red Rooster is moving up to channel eleven."

"Tin Roof to Able Mabel."

"Go Tin Roof."

"I'm not a school bus driver, but I'm pretty close by and I'd be glad to help out. Over."

"Ten-four, Tin Roof. Grab a flashlight and come on over to Lakeside, just south of Berg. When you see a school bus parked in a driveway, that's me."

By the time we reached our driveway, Mrs.

Guptill had talked to several more people. One car pulled in right behind us.

Mrs. Guptill opened the bus door. "You better get in the house and let your folks know what's happening, Davey."

As soon as I got in the kitchen, Mom and Brad came at me, both talking at the same time.

"Where have you been? We've been worried sick. You didn't even leave a note."

"You little jerk. When I get my hands on you, I'm going to break your neck!"

Brad's airplane, or what was left of it, was lying on the kitchen table.

"Uncle Will is lost in the woods," I gasped.

Dad had just come into the kitchen. "Davey! Do you have any explanation for—"

"He says Uncle Will is somewhere in the woods," Mom said.

"I tried to stay with him, but I was getting lost too."

"I told you something like this was going to happen, Jan," Dad said. "We should have done something about the situation before it was too late."

Mom pushed past Dad and put her hands on my shoulders. "This is no time for a lecture, John. Davey, do you have any idea what part of the woods Uncle Will might be in? Could he find his way back on his own?"

"No way, Mom. He thinks he's a little kid again, and he's trying to find his old home. He doesn't have any idea where he is, and I couldn't get him to come to his senses. It's all my fault. He's upset because I yelled at him for messing up Brad's plane." The minute the words were out of my mouth, I regretted them.

Brad slammed his fist down on the table. "That does it. I was almost beginning to get used to the old coot, then he goes off the deep end again. When are you people going to put him away where he belongs? Does he have to wreck the whole house first?"

"We'll discuss that later, Brad," Dad said. "Right now we need help—and fast."

I had almost forgotten about Mrs. Guptill. "We have help, Dad. Mrs. Guptill is out in the driveway in her school bus. She's already called in some other drivers on her CB radio. She's organizing a search party."

Everybody followed me back outside. There were cars lined up along the side of the road now, and people were gathering in the driveway.

A man came over to us. "I hear they're looking for somebody who's lost. Is it a kid?" he asked.

"No, it's an old man," Dad answered.

"It's both," I said under my breath.

Chapter 16

"It's wonderful that you're doing all this, Mrs. Guptill," Mom said. "But why don't you bring your radio into the kitchen where you'd be more comfortable?"

"No, thanks. I have everything I need right here, if you'd just plug this cord in somewhere." Mrs. Guptill pulled a big extension cord out of a compartment by her seat and handed it to Dad. When he plugged it into the outlet in our garage, lights went on in the bus. I got on board and slipped into the seat behind Mrs. Guptill. "Can I help look for him, Mrs. Guptill? I have my own flashlight."

Mrs. Guptill smiled. "I appreciate your wantin' to help out, Davey, but I'd rather have you stay here in Command Headquarters with me and Rooster. We may need you to run some errands for us."

A tall, red-haired man stuck his head in the door. "I rounded up quite a bunch on channel eleven, Mabel, and I have a good map of the area. What do you want me to do next?"

"Thanks, Rooster. I knew I could count on you. This here's Will's grand-nephew Davey. He'll be giving us a hand. Let's set up the table so we can spread out the map and get started." We went to the back seat of the bus, and Rooster undid something with a wrench so the seat part lifted up. Then we pulled out a big board and clamped it over the first two seats opposite the driver's side to make a table. Mrs. Guptill opened a compartment above the window and unfolded a desk lamp. Then, while Rooster spread out the map and started marking it into squares, she went to the door and called to the people who were milling around in the driveway. "Thanks for coming, everybody. Come on in and take a seat so we can give out assignments."

In a few minutes the bus was filled with people. It looked funny to see adults sitting on a school bus. I recognized a lot of the faces as bus drivers from school.

Mrs. Guptill stood up in the front of the bus. "Listen up, everybody. We're dividing the area into sections. We'll have you go out in pairs, and each pair needs to have a hand-held radio, so find your partners accordingly. We'll be operating on channel nine. When you're assigned your quadrant, first go to all of the houses along that stretch of road and get them to turn on any outside lights they have. And tell them to keep a watch for anyone coming out of the woods. You might also get some advice about the lay of the land behind their property and the best way into it."

A woman in the back of the bus raised her hand. "What if the people want to go along with us and help search?"

"That's fine, but check with me by radio first.

We need to know the name of everybody out there. No sense anybody else getting lost."

There was quite a bit of chatter starting up, and Mrs. Guptill pounded her wrench on the table to quiet them down. "Hold the chitchat. This isn't a party. We have a man lost out there. His name is Will Stark. He's seventy-four, about five-eight, medium build, white hair, and has those glasses with the wire rims."

She turned to me. "What was he wearing, Davey?"

I wasn't expecting to be called on. "Oh . . . um . . . He had on overalls and a shirt, red plaid, I think . . . no, maybe it was blue. I don't know."

"Never mind," Mrs. Guptill said. "There aren't going to be that many men matching his description running around in the woods. Didn't he have a jacket on?"

"No," I said. "I'm sure of that."

Mrs. Guptill shook her head. "That's bad. The temperature is dropping fast. All right, everybody. Get going, and stay in touch by radio. Rooster will give you your assignments as you go out."

There was a lot of confusion as the people paired up and got their assignments.

Pretty soon the last car pulled out, and the only ones left were Rooster, Mrs. Guptill, and me. Then a really familiar face came in. It was Brad.

"My dad said to tell you that he wanted to join the search, but he thinks he should stay with Mom. She's pretty upset about Uncle Will."

Mrs. Guptill nodded. "That's okay, Brad. Tell your dad we have a good-sized search party going, and more people are calling in on the radio all the time. He's needed more right where he is."

Brad didn't leave. He stood there shifting from one foot to the other while Mrs. Guptill answered another call on the radio.

". . . That's right. Lakeside, just south of Berg. Stop here, and we'll give you a map." Mrs. Guptill looked up, surprised to see Brad still standing there. "Was there something else, Brad?"

He pulled out a flashlight from his back pocket. "Well, I just thought if you needed more people . . ."

"You want to help look for your uncle?"

Brad shrugged. "Yeah, I guess. . . . Sure. I'll help."

"Great. We can always use another able-bodied man. You'll have to wait for a partner, though. There's a man due in any minute. You can team up with him."

Brad sat in the seat opposite me. He tried not to show it, but I could tell he liked the way Mrs. Guptill had called him an able-bodied man.

Mrs. Guptill was busy talking to Rooster, so I leaned over and whispered to Brad. "What do you think you're doing? You don't want them to find Uncle Will."

"Why would I be going out to look for him if I didn't want him to be found?"

"You just want to be the one to find him so you can bash him over the head with a rock and hide his body. That's how much you care."

"Geez, Davey! I'm not wild about having the old guy live with us, but I never wanted anything bad to happen to him. What do you think I am, some kind of monster?"

I glared at him. "You said it, not me."

A tall guy in a hunting jacket stepped between us. "You don't have a radio, kid?"

Brad held up the flashlight. "No sir, I don't. Just this."

"Okay. I have a rig, so you can team up with me."

Just as Brad got to the door, he turned around. "Listen, Davey. With all these people going out, we'll find him. Tell Mom not to worry." He looked as if he really meant it, but I wasn't sure. I'd never known Brad to be concerned about anybody but himself. It was especially hard to believe he cared what happened to Uncle Will.

Mrs. Guptill, Rooster, and I were only alone for a short while. Then the food started coming in. Lots of people out in the country had CB's and kept their scanners on all the time, so word of the search party got around real fast. One lady pulled up with a big coffeepot that Mrs. Guptill plugged into a hidden socket next to her seat. Then Mom came out with a platter of sandwiches, and some man dropped off a couple of big boxes of doughnuts. Finally, Mrs. Weiderman and Sara brought brownies.

"Two men just stopped by our house and said Davey's uncle is lost in the woods," Mrs. Weiderman said. "Do you have any idea which part of the woods he might be in?"

Mrs. Guptill shook her head. "He could be almost anywhere by now. We're searching the whole area bounded by the four roads, and we'll just have to hope that if he comes out on a road and crosses it, somebody will see him."

Sara and I slid into a seat near the back of the bus, and Mrs. Weiderman went into the house to talk to my parents.

Mrs. Guptill and Rooster were busy directing the search over the radio, so they didn't pay any attention to us.

"What happened?" Sara whispered. "How did he get lost?"

I told her the whole thing.

"He'll be all right, Davey. They'll find him," Sara said when I had finished.

"Yeah, but even if they do, I don't think Mom and Dad are going to let him stay with us much longer because he's causing too much trouble. Mom said if things didn't work out here, he'd have to go to a nursing home."

"That's terrible. He's fine most of the time, isn't he?"

"Yeah, he's great, except when he gets mixed up or thinks he's Willie."

"There must be some other place he could live," Sara said.

"Sure, but how do we find it?"

Sara got up and started pacing. After about fourteen trips up and down the aisle, she slid back into the seat. "I've got it," she whispered. "We'll run an ad in the *Penny Pincher.*" She pulled a pencil and paper out of her pocket and started writing.

"Elderly man needs place to live," she began.

"I don't like *elderly,*" I whispered. "It makes it sound like he's all crippled up or something."

Sara bit on her pencil. "I know what you mean. *Old* is bad too. How about *mature?* Mature gentleman?"

"Not *gentleman*. Uncle Will never wears anything fancier than farmer's overalls. Try *mature farmer.*"

Sara erased the beginning and started over. " 'Mature farmer needs place to live.' No. That sounds too desperate."

"He is desperate," I said.

"Yes, but you don't want people to know that. This sounds like he's standing out in the street with his suitcase, for Pete's sake. How about 'Mature farmer seeks new living arrangements'?"

"Yeah, that's good," I said. "But you need to say something good about him, otherwise why would anyone let him move in?"

"All right. What are his good points?"

"Well, he has a great sense of humor, and he likes kids . . . and he knows everything there is to know about chickens."

"Mmm," Sara said, writing it all down. "Okay, listen to this. 'Mature farmer with great sense of humor seeks new living arrangements. Is good with kids and chickens.' "

"Yeah, that's okay, except for one thing."

Sara was getting impatient. "What now, Davey?"

"Well, I don't think it's right not to mention that he thinks he's a little kid sometimes. I mean, if he didn't keep getting mixed up, he wouldn't be seeking new living arrangements in the first place."

Sara chewed on her eraser. "That's true, but we can't come right out and say he thinks he's a little kid. They never put bad stuff in ads unless they disguise it. Once my father put in an ad for an old car that wouldn't run at all. He just said, 'Engine needs some work.' "

She wrote something else. "Listen to this. 'Mature farmer with great sense of humor seeks new living arrangements. Good with children and chickens. Has youthful outlook.' "

"Perfect! Just add our phone number, and you've got it."

Just then, Mrs. Weiderman came out to the bus. "Come on, Sara," she called. "It's getting late."

"Oh, Mom, couldn't I stay with Davey until they find Mr. Stark?" Sara asked.

"No. We really have to leave now."

Sara slipped me the piece of paper with the ad on it. "Be sure and send this in to the *Penny Pincher,* Davey," she whispered.

I tucked it into my pocket and walked Sara out to the car. The moon was full again, just like it had been last month when Uncle Will and I had murdered the zucchinis, only it was much colder tonight. I remembered what Uncle Will had said about a killing frost, and shivered.

"Do you really think that ad will work, Sara?" I whispered.

Sara shrugged. "I don't know. My father never did sell that old Ford."

Chapter 17

I climbed onto the bus and went to the back seat. Mrs. Guptill was giving orders over her radio. "Ten-four, Quadrant Seven. If your whole section has been covered, I want you to move on to Quadrant Thirteen. That starts at 674 County Line Road and runs south to 583."

I curled up in the back corner and pulled the ad out of my pocket. I read it to myself. It still sounded great. I was sure there was some family out there who would read it and take in Uncle Will. But then I realized something. What I really wanted was to find a way to convince my family that he should stay with us. I figured Mom might be on my side, him being her favorite uncle and all, but I couldn't imagine how we'd ever win over Brad and Dad. I folded the paper back up and held it in my hand as I fell asleep to the crackling of Mrs. Guptill's radio.

I woke up a few times during the night, as groups of searchers came back to warm up with coffee and food. Then I'd fall asleep again and have terrible dreams. In one, I was chasing Uncle Will through the woods, and it started to snow. It got harder and harder to run as the snow piled up, and he was moving farther ahead of me. I was just about ready to give up and go back when I saw him fall down.

I kept going, struggling to get to him, but the snow was clumping up on my sneakers until I could hardly put one foot in front of the other. When I finally reached him, he was buried in about a foot of snow. I dug with my bare hands, and when I uncovered his face, it had turned to ice—not just frozen flesh, but ice that you could see clear through.

Somehow, I managed to get him to his feet and help him walk through the snow all the way back to our house. When we got there, I put a chair right next to the wood stove for him so he could warm up. But he didn't warm up. He just melted away, until all that was left was a pile of soggy clothes in the chair and a puddle of water on the floor.

Suddenly a loud roar woke me up. We were moving! As Mrs. Guptill gunned the bus out of our driveway, I rolled off the seat onto the floor. I struggled to my feet and hung on to the seats on both sides as I made my way to the front. Rooster was manning the radio. "We're on our way, Quadrant Fifteen. How does he look?"

A crackly voice came back. "He's dazed and he's half froze, Red Rooster, but he was on his feet when we found him. He needs to be checked over by a doctor, though."

"Ten-four, Quadrant Fifteen. We'll take him on in to Emergency at General." Rooster patted Mrs. Guptill on the back. "Sounds like Will's going to be okay, Mabel."

I could see her face in the rear-view mirror. She had tears in her eyes, but when she looked up and saw me, she wiped them away quickly with the back of her hand. "Davey? I forgot you were on board. They found your uncle Will. We're going to pick him up now."

"I know. I heard. That's really terrific."

"We'll be needing some blankets and a pillow, Davey. Go back and lift up the seat under the Baltimore oriole. You should find what you need in there. Rooster, you can get the bed set up."

Rooster went to work with the wrench again, and by the time we reached Quadrant Fifteen, he had flipped over a few of the seats, dug another board out of the back to clamp over them, and put a thin mattress over the whole thing. "Wow, that's neat," I said.

Rooster threw a blanket on the mattress. "Yep, Mabel converts this bus into a camper in the summertime, and she travels all over the country. Just puts the seats back in each year after Labor Day."

Mrs. Guptill brought the bus to a lurching stop and opened the door. "Bring him on in. We have a bed ready."

Uncle Will appeared in the doorway. He looked pale and confused, like a frightened animal caught in a trap. Mrs. Guptill got up and took hold of his hands. "Come on, Will. It's me, Mabel."

Somebody steadied him from behind as he started to step up into the bus. Uncle Will looked right at me, but didn't seem to know who I was.

The guy behind Uncle Will was trying to help

him climb up. "Easy, Uncle Will. There's just one more step, but it's a big one." It was Brad again.

"Were you the ones who found him?" I asked.

Brad stepped out of the way and let Rooster take over with Uncle Will. "No," Brad said. "We were in the next quadrant over, so when we heard on the radio that they found him, we ran over to help." Maybe Brad cared after all.

Mrs. Guptill and Rooster eased Uncle Will down into the bed. "You take over the wheel, Rooster. I'll stay with Will on the trip in. You'd better get on the rig and thank everybody for helping out, and have Quadrant One do a roll call to make sure they get all the searchers back in." She turned to Uncle Will and smiled, tucking the blanket around him. "Will? You're going to be all right, you hear? You're safe now."

Uncle Will looked scared. He jerked one hand out from under the blanket and tried to rub it across his forehead. The hand was stiff and shaking so much he almost poked himself in the eye.

Mrs. Guptill took his hand in hers and rubbed it briskly. "There, there, now, Will. You'll feel much better when we get you thawed out. Get an extra blanket on him, Brad. And Davey, take his other hand and see if you can't warm it up some."

Brad put a blanket around him, and I reached over to get his hand. It felt like a package of hamburger that had just come out of the freezer.

"Do my parents know you found Uncle Will, Mrs. Guptill?" Brad asked.

"Tarnation! In all the excitement, I forgot to tell them. Rooster!"

"Yeah?"

"Have somebody go over to the Andersons' and tell them what's happening. They can meet us at the hospital."

"Ten-four, Able Mabel."

Brad went to the front of the bus. "I can do that if you want, Rooster. Mr. Jenkins showed me how to work his radio."

A weak smile flickered across Uncle Will's face.

"What is it, Will?" Mrs. Guptill asked. "You want to tell us something?"

He whispered something, too softly for us to hear.

"What was that, Will?"

We both leaned closer. His words came out in a little puff of breath. "Able Mabel," he said and smiled again before he closed his eyes.

We raised a real commotion when Rooster pulled the school bus into the ambulance entrance at the hospital. People in white uniforms started running toward us from every direction. I guess they thought they had a major school-bus disaster on their hands. Some of them seemed a little disappointed to find out it was just one old man, but at least Uncle Will got a lot of extra attention. When they took him out on a stretcher, Mrs. Guptill went along. I wanted to go with them, but she said it would be best if Brad and I stayed on the bus with Rooster until they got Uncle Will settled.

About fifteen minutes later, Mom and Dad pulled up in the parking lot and went running inside. Not long after that, Mrs. Guptill came back out to the bus.

"I thought you'd stay with Will for a while," Rooster said. "How's he doing?"

"He's going to be fine, but he's got his family with him now. I'm going to take the boys in. You and I can see him after he gets home, Rooster."

"How soon is he going home, Mrs. Guptill?" I asked.

"I don't know, Davey. Not just yet. They want to keep an eye on him for a bit."

As we walked into the emergency room, I thought about how I'd try to make things easier for Uncle Will when he got home. I'd try to pay more attention to him and invite him along to do things with Sara and me. Sara understood him and liked him as much as I did. I knew we could make it work. The sun was starting to come up, making the bottoms of the clouds turn pink.

Mom met us in the waiting room. "Thank you so much for everything, Mrs. Guptill. John and I really appreciate all your help."

"No need thanking me, Mrs. Anderson. Will's a good friend. He'd do the same for me if the tables were turned. I'll come see him when he gets home."

Mom looked flustered. "Well, yes, of course, that is, if—"

Dad interrupted and reached past Mom to shake hands with Mrs. Guptill. "You're welcome in our home any time, Mrs. Guptill. Thanks again."

Mrs. Guptill smiled, but she had a funny expression on her face as she headed for the door.

"Where is Uncle Will, Mom?" I asked.

"Follow me. I'll show you." We went around the corner into a big room that had a lot of curtained-off spaces with narrow padded tables in them. A few of the cubicles had the curtains pulled all the way around in front so you couldn't see who was inside.

"He's in that cubicle over there," Mom said, pointing to one that was closed off. I could see a couple of pairs of feet sticking out under the curtain, but neither of them was Uncle Will's. The space next to Uncle Will was open, and the guy in there was lying real still. I thought he might be dead. Then Uncle Will's curtain was shoved back, and a doctor and nurse came out.

Mom went right up to the doctor. "Doctor? I'm Janet Anderson, Will Stark's niece. How is he doing?"

He shook hands with Mom and Dad. "Glad to meet you. I'm Dr. Blanchard. Your uncle is doing very well, but we felt it was best to observe him for a few hours. I think he should be ready for release by noon. He's a very strong man for his age."

I was trying to see around them into Uncle Will's cubicle, but his head was facing the other way, so all I could see were his stocking feet sticking out from under the blanket.

Mom was twisting the strap to her purse. "Well, yes, physically he's fine. It's just that he's . . . well . . . Doctor, is there someplace we could go to talk?"

"Certainly. We can use the conference room just down the hall." He paused, then looked at Mom. "Are your sons coming with us?"

"No. I think they'd rather go in to see Uncle Will, if that would be all right."

The doctor smiled. "That's fine. Go ahead, boys. But remember, he's had quite an ordeal, and he's a bit confused at the moment. So don't tire him out."

"Okay. We won't," Brad said.

Uncle Will looked pale, and at first I thought he was asleep, but he opened his eyes when I got close to him. Brad stayed back by the curtain.

"Hi, Uncle Will," I whispered. "Are you okay?"

"I guess so."

"I'm sorry I yelled at you," I said.

He just looked at me through half-open eyes and didn't say anything, so I kept talking. "The doctor says maybe you can go home by noon. I was afraid they'd make you stay longer. You were in the woods a long time."

"Woods?" He blinked a few times, then opened his eyes all the way.

"Don't you remember? You went way back into the woods and got lost."

"No. Can't say as I do." Uncle Will rubbed his chin. Little silver bristles were starting to show, because he hadn't shaved since yesterday morning.

Brad came over to Uncle Will. "You were lost almost all night, and Mrs. Guptill was in charge of the search party. She ran the whole thing from the bus with her CB radio. They call her Able Mabel."

"No kidding. Mabel did that for me? She's quite a woman." He shook his head, smiling. "Able Mabel, you say. That's a good name for her."

"Yeah. Don't you remember?" I asked. "You called her that on the bus coming in."

I was sorry I said that, because his face got serious again. "It bothers me when I can't remember things. My mind just don't work right sometimes. It's been happening a lot lately. Your mother gets upset with me when I forget things on the stove. She's right. I guess I do forget."

"You could tie a string around your finger when you put the water on so you'd remember to turn it off," I said.

"What would I use to remind me what the string was for?" Uncle Will asked, waiting a second or two before he broke into a grin. He chuckled to himself for a minute.

Then his face got serious again. "I'm afraid it's all over for me, Davey. I'm on my way out."

"What are you talking about, Uncle Will? You're not dying. The doctor says you're real strong for a man your age."

"My body may be strong, but my mind keeps playing tricks on me." His eyes started to look watery. "I should be put away in one of them old folks' homes where they can keep an eye on me."

Brad looked embarrassed and backed away. "Look, I'm really starved, so I'm going to check out the cafeteria. Hang in there, Uncle Will, okay?" Brad took off before either of us could say anything.

I reached over and took Uncle Will's hand. "Listen, Uncle Will. You belong with us. It's going to be okay. You can hang out with me and Sara and we'll—"

Just then a nurse came in. "I'm afraid I'm going to have to ask you to leave, young man. Mr. Stark needs to get some rest."

"Okay," I said. "I'll go look for Mom and Dad, Uncle Will. They'll tell you everything is fine, so don't worry."

I walked down the hall until I found a door

labeled CONFERENCE ROOM. The door was open a little bit, so I could see Mom and Dad sitting at a table with the doctor.

The doctor was talking. "From what you're telling me, it sounds as if it might be Alzheimer's disease. Of course, tests would have to be run to rule out other possibilities."

I knocked and poked my head in. "Hi," I said. "Can I come in?"

Dad cleared his throat but didn't say anything, and Mom looked down at her hands. I could tell she'd been crying.

The doctor stood up. "I'll leave the three of you alone so you can . . . ah . . . talk. We'll go ahead with the plan. I'll start making arrangements." He picked up some papers and hurried out of the room.

"What plan?" I asked, sliding into a seat across from Mom and Dad. "Listen, you have to talk to Uncle Will because he feels real bad and thinks he has to go into a home for old people."

Mom's hands started talking before she did. "You're going to have to understand that what we're doing is in Uncle Will's best interests, Davey. We just want him to be happy and comfortable . . . and safe."

"Safe from what?" I asked.

"Safe from himself, really. When we described Uncle Will's behavior to the doctor, he agreed that this is the kindest thing to do."

"What's going on? You sound like you're going to have him put to sleep."

"Davey," Dad said. "Never mind the smart remarks. This isn't easy for your mother."

Mom took a deep breath. "The doctor said that Uncle Will's confusion will probably get worse, and there really isn't anything they can do to treat it. They can't admit him to this hospital because he has a chronic condition."

"What does that mean?" I asked.

"A chronic condition is one that won't go away," Dad answered.

"You mean like Brad?" I joked, but neither of them even smiled.

Mom kept on talking. "We don't know for sure yet, but it sounds as if Uncle Will might have Alzheimer's disease. At any rate, we do know that he's going to need constant supervision. We just can't give him that at home."

"Sure we can, Mom. There are four of us. We can take turns. Well, not Brad, maybe. But the three of us can watch him . . . and Sara, too."

"No, Davey. That sounds like a nice idea, but it isn't practical."

I couldn't believe it. After all this talk about Uncle Will being her favorite uncle, even Mom was going to give up on him? She was just going to write him off and not even try to figure out a way to take care of him? It was all happening too fast. Mom was still babbling on, with her hands in overdrive.

". . . and so when Dr. Blanchard told us it would be much easier to get him into a nursing home if we transferred him directly from the hospital . . . and he thought they might have a bed available at Cottonwood Nursing Home . . . well, it made so much more sense than taking him home and putting him on a waiting list that might take six months to a year, so we told him to go ahead."

"Right into a nursing home from here? Aren't we even going to take Uncle Will home with us?" I cried. "We can work things out at home, Mom. Maybe Uncle Will will get better if we just give him a little more time."

"It's out of our hands, Davey," Dad said. "The papers have been signed."

"I don't care about any stupid papers," I yelled. "You can't put Uncle Will away in some old nursing home. He belongs with people who love him. That's what you said when you brought him home to live with us, Mom. Why is it different now?"

"When we brought Uncle Will to Adams, I had no idea how severe his problem was," Mom said.

"So just because he has a problem, you want to dump him? You didn't get rid of Kaiser when you found out he was deaf, and you kept that stupid chicken that still runs around in circles."

Mom reached across the table to take my hand. "Davey, Uncle Will has changed. Try to understand. He just isn't the Will Stark I knew and loved."

I pulled my hand away and jumped up. "Well, I didn't know the old Will Stark," I shouted. "But I love the person he is now."

"I couldn't have said it better myself, Davey." We all turned toward the voice at the door.

"Mrs. Guptill," Mom said. "I didn't realize you were still here."

Mrs. Guptill held up a little folded piece of paper.

"I found your ad where you dropped it on the

back seat of the bus, Davey," she said. "And I've come in answer to it. For years I've been wanting to find a mature farmer with a youthful outlook."

Mom looked puzzled. "An ad? I'm afraid I don't understand."

Mrs. Guptill grinned and tucked the paper down the front of her dress. "Don't fret over it, honey. It's an inside joke. Come on, Davey."

Mrs. Guptill grabbed my arm and dragged me right past Mom and Dad, down the hall to Uncle Will's cubicle in the emergency room. She yanked back the curtain and stood at the foot of his bed with her hands on her hips. "Will Stark," she said in her big gruff voice. "Will you marry me?"

Uncle Will's mouth dropped open. "Mabel? Is that you?"

"Well, who else do you know that might be proposin' to you? What's your answer? Do you want to marry me or not?"

Uncle Will looked sad and tired. "I'm an old man, Mabel. Too old to think about gettin' hitched up."

"Who in tarnation's been putting that nonsense into your head? I don't want to marry some green sixty-year-old kid. I want to marry you."

Uncle Will smiled. "I appreciate what you're tryin' to do, Mabel, but—"

"I'm givin' you one more chance, Will Stark. You have a choice between living out your days in a nursing home or a future filled with love, laughter, and walnut squares. What'll it be? Will you marry me or not?"

Uncle Will laughed. "You bet I will, Able Mabel." He held his arms out to her.

Mrs. Guptill went over to Uncle Will and kissed him. Right on the mouth! Sara wasn't going to believe this. People all over the emergency room began to clap, even the corpse in the next cubicle. And somebody yelled, "Right on, funky mama!"

Mom and Dad had been right behind us, and Dr. Blanchard came out from behind one of the curtains. "What's all the commotion here? This is a hospital. We can't have this."

Mrs. Guptill was holding Uncle Will's hand in both of hers. "You're going to have to cancel that nursing home reservation for Will Stark, Doc," she said. "He's going to need honeymoon reservations instead."

Mom looked like she was directing an orchestra. "Dr. Blanchard, I think we need to go back into the conference room so you can explain Uncle Will's prognosis to Mrs. Guptill."

Mrs. Guptill stood up straight. "I heard all that when I was standing outside the door, and I think you're all full of horsefeathers."

Dr. Blanchard was coming toward Mrs. Guptill the way a policeman pussyfoots up to a crazy person with a gun. "Now, Mrs. Guptill. If you will just come with me . . ."

"We aren't going anywhere, Doc. Will needs to hear this, too. Did anyone bother to tell you what's happened to this man in the past six months? About his brother dying and all?"

Doctor Blanchard stopped and looked at Mom. "Why, no. I didn't realize there had been a death in the family."

I took Uncle Will's other hand. "Yeah. Uncle Will and his brother, Ray, ran their farm all by themselves," I said. "He really misses Ray, and he's sad about the farm going up for auction, too."

Dr. Blanchard's eyebrows shot up. "This man has just lost a loved one and he's had to leave his farm? His whole way of life has changed?"

Mom looked as if somebody had just slapped her in the face. "Well, we try not to talk about it at home, for Uncle Will's sake. And I didn't mention it to you because it didn't have anything to do with the . . . the present problem."

"My dear woman," Dr. Blanchard said. "It has everything to do with the problem. It totally changes the picture. It would be perfectly natural for a man who had gone through that much of an upheaval in his life to show all kinds of mental strain. This man has been trying to deal with grief—and depression too, no doubt."

"You got it, Doc," Mrs. Guptill said. "When I lost my Louie, I darn near went crazy. Didn't even know who I was half the time. But I came out of it, and Will here will too. Besides, just because a body gets mixed up once in a while doesn't mean he belongs in a nursing home. My neighbor, old Morris Bronswiller, thinks he's the Lone Ranger, but nobody's putting him away. They just let him sit on his porch wearing his little black mask and yelling 'Hi-yo Silver, away!,' and go on about their business." She turned to the crowd of people that had gathered around. "What's everybody staring at? Somebody find this man his shoes. We have to get ready for a wedding."

Chapter 18

The wedding date was set for the following Saturday. Uncle Will spent every day that week with Mrs. Guptill, just coming home to sleep. He seemed happier than I'd ever seen him, and said that they were working "on a project."

The day of the wedding finally arrived. Uncle Will had chosen me to be his best man, so I had to keep track of the ring. I was also supposed to help him get ready. I heard him humming in the bathroom that morning, but the door was open, so I looked in.

"Wow," I said. "You look great. I didn't know you had a good suit like that."

Uncle Will was wetting his hair and combing it across his forehead, trying to anchor the part that always fell down. His face was all shiny, and he smelled of Dad's after-shave.

"I got this suit for Ray's funeral. Thought the next time I'd need it would be for my own. Now look at me. A bridegroom for the first time at seventy-four." He grinned and turned around in a circle like a model. The hunk of hair slowly slid back down on his forehead.

"Yeah," I said. "You look terrific." I felt in my pocket for the ring for about the hundredth time.

Uncle Will and Mrs. Guptill (Aunt Mabel, now) had the neatest wedding I'd ever seen. I almost didn't recognize Aunt Mabel when she came down the aisle at the church. She was wearing a long blue dress and had a wreath of flowers in her hair. Uncle Will didn't seem nervous at all. When it came to the part where he was supposed to say, "I do," he said, "You're durn right I do," and his voice boomed out over the whole church.

The best part came after the ceremony, when we went to the reception at the school. They had a band in the gym and a ton of food that Aunt Mabel's bus-driver friends brought.

Then we all went out in the parking lot, and the other drivers did a twenty-one bus salute for the wedding couple. They lined the buses up in a huge figure eight that took up the whole parking lot. When Mr. Stickle, the head of Transportation, blew his whistle, they started moving. At the center of the 8 where the two lines crossed, the buses took turns passing in front of each other with just inches to spare, a maneuver they'd been practicing for the School Bus Drivers' Rodeo. Aunt Mabel had tears in her eyes when she watched them. So did Mr. Stickle, but I think he was worried that somebody might have spiked the punch.

"Davey," Aunt Mabel called when the buses had finished their routine. "Come over here and bring Sara. I want to show you something."

She led us over to the bus, which I wouldn't have recognized because now the outside was painted white with rainbow-colored racing stripes down the sides.

"It's beautiful, Mrs. Guptill—I mean Mrs. Stark," Sara said. "But won't the school get mad at you for painting the outside? It doesn't look like a school bus anymore."

"That's because it isn't a school bus anymore," Aunt Mabel said. "Come see the inside."

It sure wasn't a school bus. It was a house, just like those big motor homes we saw once at the Trailer Show. There were two seats in the front—fancy ones with plush red velvet seat covers—then a little kitchen on one side and a table with benches on the other. Behind that was a living room with a couch on each side, then a big bed and a closed-off section for the bathroom. Aunt Mabel sat down on one of the couches, and Sara and I sat across from her.

"Fancy, ain't it?" Aunt Mabel said, running her hand over a soft velvet cushion.

"Who did all this?" I asked.

"Me, Will, Rooster, and a lot of the other drivers. We worked on it nonstop all week." She looked up at the ceiling and laughed. A few strands of her hair pulled out of the wreath and fell down over her face. "We painted over everything else, but Will wanted to leave the clouds and stars. He said they made a nice decoration."

Sara looked up. "Yes, they do. But aren't you going to be a school-bus driver anymore, Mrs. Stark?"

"Nope," Aunt Mabel said. "I only did that to have something to do. Didn't really need the money.

I have some mighty good friends here, though. I'm going to miss them."

"Miss them?" I said. "You aren't going away, are you?"

"We're just taking a trip for a few months or so. We'll start out with Florida, then probably swing out west."

"You think Uncle Will is well enough to go off on a trip, Aunt Mabel? What if he still has times when he thinks he's a little kid?"

"He might, for a while, but that won't be a problem. And I'm sure he'll come out of it, sooner or later. Didn't I tell you about the dollhouse I built after my Louie died?"

"You had a dollhouse?" I asked. It was hard to picture Mrs. Guptill playing with dolls.

"Yep. Ain't that somethin'? I shut myself off from everybody and set about making a dollhouse. I made furniture for all the rooms and even carved out a little family to put in it."

"Who were you making it for?" Sara asked.

"I didn't really know at the time, but I was making it for myself. It was a kind of therapy, I guess. My kids were all grown and moved away with families of their own, and I didn't want to move in with any of them. But with Louie gone, I couldn't stand the loneliness. So I made a little imaginary home to live in, with a family to keep me company."

"That's weird," I said. "Did you talk to the dolls?"

Sara had a fit. "Davey! That's none of our business."

Aunt Mabel laughed. "That's okay, Sara. Sure, I

talked to them. I could almost hear them talking back to me. I told you, I was nuttier than a fruitcake."

"But how did you get better?" I asked.

She leaned back and smiled. "Time helped. And stubborn friends like Rooster and his wife, who kept bugging me until I started going out some. But I still worked away at that dollhouse, cutting and gluing and wallpapering the little walls, just keeping busy so I could work out the pain. And then one day, I knew the dollhouse had done its job. I put it away and started living in the real world again."

"That's amazing," Sara said.

"That's what Will's going to do, too."

"Build a dollhouse?" I asked.

Sara rolled her eyes, so I figured I'd said something dumb.

Aunt Mabel laughed. "Probably not, Davey. But he'll find his own way to work out his pain. Sometimes I think that's what he's doing when he acts like a little boy, or a teenager. He's taking himself back to happier times."

"A teenager? He never did that with me," I said. "What do you do when that happens?"

Aunt Mabel threw her head back and laughed, making more strands of hair pull away from the wreath. She was beginning to look more like herself. "What do I do? I enjoy every minute of it. When he's sixteen, I'm sixteen. There's a lot to be said for living in a fantasy world once in a while, Davey. Reality is all right, but I like a little rest from it every now and then. Will gives me that."

"Then it's okay with you that he gets a little

confused and you'll probably have to watch him a lot?"

"He's a lot easier to watch than a bus load of you kids," she said. "Besides, I love the man. Come on. Let's get back to the party."

There was a lot more dancing and eating, then Aunt Mabel and Uncle Will cut the wedding cake and she threw her bouquet. Mom kept crying and saying things like, "Oh, isn't it wonderful. They seem so happy together." She really bawled when Uncle Will asked the band to play a waltz. He went up to her and bowed, and they did one of their old Stark Follies routines together. As a waltzer, he wasn't half bad, in spite of the little hitch when he stepped on his right leg.

Even Brad seemed to be having a good time at the wedding. One of Aunt Mabel's granddaughter's was his age, and a real looker. When they weren't hanging around the punch bowl together, they were dancing—the fast stuff, not the waltzes. The poor girl had all she could do to stay out of the way of Brad's monster feet.

Finally it was time for Uncle Will and Aunt Mabel to leave, and we all went out into the parking lot to see them off. Uncle Will gave me a big hug. "I'll miss you, boy. But we won't be gone too long. You and me need to get an early start on those zucchinis next spring, before they get out of hand." He winked at me, then he and Aunt Mabel climbed into the bus and started off.

Aunt Mabel did a grand slalom down the full length of the parking lot, blowing her horn in the rhythm of "Here Comes the Bride." Everybody waved